Satan's Saddlemate

Satan's Saddlemate

RAY NOLAN

A Black Horse Western

ROBERT HALE · LONDON

© Ray Nolan 1998
First published in Great Britain 1998

ISBN 0 7090 6206 0

Robert Hale Limited
Clerkenwell House
Clerkenwell Green
London EC1R 0HT

Photoset in North Wales by
Derek Doyle & Associates, Mold, Flintshire.
Printed and bound in Great Britain by
WBC Book Manufacturers Limited, Bridgend.

For

MIKE GROSS

A valued friend and an exceptionally talented broadcaster, whose radio show, *Swingin' West*, brings such enjoyment to so many.

1

Not yet drunk, but well on his way to getting there, Lance McQuade, slouched over a table in the Ten Spot, barely conscious of the muted voices at the bar. He reached again for the bottle, and through a tangle of dark thoughts surfaced a sharp reminder.

It was mid-week, and late, and the old man was going to raise all kinds of hell when he and the others got back to Slash.

A husky round-faced boy, his attire flashier, more expensive than the average cowman could afford, McQuade refilled his glass, trying to recall what they'd been doing here in town. Something about a meeting of cattlemen his father had insisted he attend, picking up wire and new windmill rods.

Squinting along the length of the bar he could see only three men, Mel Tavener in the middle. Vaguely he remembered a couple of Tavener's attempts to get him headed back home.

Then he was hearing again snatches of loud talk at the meeting and the squealing of those damned ragtag outfits, complaining about torn-down fences and stock driven off. Without being conscious of it, he was giggling. Let the stupid bastards howl: there was nothing else they could do. Nobody'd ever pin anything like that on Slash. Hell, he and the old man were too damn smart for any of them.

Suddenly conscious of eyes upon him, he choked back the sounds he was making. The three at the bar returned to their drinks, Tavener muttering something he could not hear, but which brought a guffaw from one of the others.

Glass still clutched in his fist, McQuade rose angrily and kicked back his chair. They were talking about him, he had no doubt of that.

Unsteadily, he started forward, halting when what seemed like a large shadow passed in front of him. Only then did he become aware of the funereal silence that had descended upon the saloon.

He'd not heard the swing of the batwings, nor a footfall upon the hard floor, yet there was now a fourth at the bar, standing well apart from the others, and only a few feet away from where he'd stopped. A tall man; a wide-shouldered, unsmiling man whose presence laid a frost on Lance McQuade's heart and almost sobered him.

O'Grady . . . .

Tavener and the pair with him watched from the corners of their eyes, but the new arrival treated them as if they weren't there. Picking up the beer, slid across the mahogany by the bartender, he tasted it, put it back on the wood, and began fashioning a cigarette. In the midst of doing so, he turned, fastening his gaze upon McQuade.

'Glad you're still here,' he said quietly.

The boy swallowed, eyes dropping to O'Grady's hips. Finding no gun there, realizing that three of his crew were on hand should he need them, he drew back his shoulders, tried to pull himself up straight, and almost lost his balance.

'That right?'

O'Grady nodded. 'Thought we might talk about you and Gil. And a lady who'll not be named in a place like this.'

McQuade felt his face stiffen, the coldness in his chest slide down to his stomach.

'Don't know what you're talkin' about.'

A match scraped against wood.

'You're dumb, Lance, but you can't be that stupid.'

'Lay off the kid,' Tavener's voice cut in. 'He's been drinking; doesn't know which end's up.'

O'Grady ignored him. Eyes hardening upon McQuade, he took another slow drag on the quirly. 'Want to try again?'

Encouraged by Tavener's intervention, McQuade's full lips made an ugly twist.

'All right! Don't know what th' hell she's told you, but it's a damn lie!' A hand lifted. He glanced at it as if surprised to find fingers still wrapped around a glass.

O'Grady pushed slowly away from the bar, narrowing the gap between them. A thin stream of smoke broke up against McQuade's face.

'That any way to talk about a lady?'

McQuade moved his head, started to say something, changed his mind, and downed the drink in a single gulp. As he let the glass fall his hand dropped to the butt of his gun.

'I'll talk as I damn please,' he snarled, reaching forward with his left to move aside that which blocked his path. 'Now get th' hell outa my way.'

'When I'm through.' And McQuade's arm was knocked rudely aside.

Recalling a similar indignation only days past, Lance McQuade swore, and brought up a right that dropped before getting anywhere near its intended target. A backhand blow had come up from somewhere, slashing across his face, sending him backpedalling into the recently vacated table. The bottle from which he'd been drinking struck the floor and went rolling.

Tavener dipped for his own gun, but froze when he saw that someone had, a moment before, pushed through the swing doors and was now standing there, staring.

By some miracle McQuade stayed on his feet, shook his head, muttered something no one could understand, and lunged.

A fist stopped him in his tracks, and again he went flying backwards, only this time his legs failed him. As he folded to the floor there was once more the sound of doors flapping closed.

Tavener cast a quick glance in that direction, saw that the party who'd been there moments ago had apparently decided not to stay. Again he reached for his gun, hesitating when a cry of unfettered fury tore through the saloon.

Lance McQuade was climbing back onto his legs, clawing clumsily for the ivory-handled gun in its silver-studded sheath.

Before the weapon could clear leather, knuckles smashed into his face, and for the third time he was sent spinning, this time to land in a heap close to the bar.

Mel Tavener was fisting his Colt now, knowing he had to stop what was happening, but not sure of the best way to do it.

Twisting on to his side, McQuade made a swipe at his nose, saw blood on the back of his hand, and came up from the floor with a speed that surprised even Tavener. Lips peeled back, eyes threatening to burst from his skull, he made another grab at his holster, spewing curses when finding that somehow it had emptied; in a lunatic rage, he charged his opponent who stood waiting, his expression unchanged from what it was when he first entered the Ten Spot.

McQuade was still moving when one of his boots came down hard on the bottle that had fallen from his table. His body appeared to lift a few inches, and then he was going down like a structure having its foundation blown out from under. The side of his head struck the corner post of the brass rail, and then he was perfectly still.

Which was when the gun in Tavener's hand lifted high, arcing down with all the force its owner could muster.

O'Grady opened his eyes to find men bunched around him, all talking at the same time. Some of the jabbering got through to him . . . something about a fractured skull. Pain knifing through his head when he tried to sit up made him wonder if they were referring to him.

He heard the sheriff shouting for silence, but before receiving it Mel Tavener made his voice heard.

'Damnit, Prentice, you been told what happened! Lock the bastard up! He came in squaring for trouble. He started in on the kid, knowing he was too drunk to fight. All of us seen it.'

'That's right,' another said nervously. 'That's exactly how it was.' It sounded like Gus Robey, the bartender.

'Shut up!' Dan Prentice yelled, and in a milder tone addressed the man trying to get up from the saloon floor. 'You hit him?'

Instead of answering, O'Grady hauled himself upright, using the bar for support. Close to where he'd been sprawled lay Lance McQuade. Someone had draped a cloth over his head. Probably Doc Brophy, who stood by the body, a deep, disapproving frown on his ruddy face.

'I asked a question,' Prentice said, voice growing tight.

O'Grady nodded, wincing when pain exploded behind his eyes.

'When he went for his gun, yes – I hit him.' He tried to expain how McQuade had come at him again, how he'd stepped on the bottle and taken a backward flip.

'What bottle?' Tavener shouted. 'What gun? You see any gun?'

O'Grady's gaze shifted slowly back to the body on the floor. McQuade was no longer wearing the fancy gunrig.

'I tell you he came in here hunting trouble!' Tavener was still talking fast and loud. 'The kid didn't stand a chance, not in the condition he was.'

The sheriff turned to someone standing on the inner edge of the group, a man in a dark grey broadcloth suit and bright-blue vest.

'You see any of it, Carl?'

Carl Pickard, owner of the Ten Spot, solemnly shook his head.

'I was in my office. Came out to see what was going on, and found the boy already dead.'

'See a bottle on the floor? Any sign of a gun?'

Pickard's head moved again. 'Afraid not.'

2

Knowing he was on the last leg of his journey home should have brought some feeling of pleasant anticipation. Instead, with each jolt and lurch of the stage, O'Grady felt only the slow stirring of apprehension.

It had been two years since he'd seen Tailgate, and he had no idea what welcome awaited him there. He didn't know if Shamrock would still be his to go back to.

He shifted his long frame into a more comfortable position, thinking yet again of the letter from the Cattleman's Bank, informing him of an offer received for the ranch. A long while later there'd been a second letter, that one registering disappointment at his decision, adding that, under present circumstances, and the fact that his liquid capital was almost exhausted, his stance should be seriously reconsidered. That was six months ago, and again he'd said no. After that there'd been nothing.

Two letters in that many years.

Not once had Stacey written. Not that he'd expected her to. But a man hopes. If only for a while.

From the window at his left, he watched the familiar Monroe County landscape slip by, fading under a rapidly thickening cloak of grey, remembering that

13

last morning in Tailgate, waiting, hoping she'd come to say goodbye. And maybe just one of the things he needed to hear from her.

He was still waiting when her uncle stopped awkwardly before him.

'Stacey won't be coming, if that's what you're perhaps hoping for.'

'Your idea, Dan?'

'Figured it best she keep away,' Dan Prentice muttered, wheeling back to his office.

On the opposite seat a slight built man in a travel-rumpled suit was looking at his watch.

'Should be there in another couple of hours.'

Neither of the other passengers made any response. Since boarding the stage only the man now putting away the timepiece had made any attempt at conversation.

The Concord was moving slower as it started up the broad pass that would take them through the Sentinels. It would be dark before they hit town, which suited O'Grady just fine. That way there was less chance of running into anyone he knew.

At the top of the pass where the road levelled off, the ground rose up steeply on both sides until it was like travelling through a high-vaulted tunnel. The driver brought the team to a walk, allowing the animals to blow, preparing them for the long descent and the final run.

Eventually the wide-slopes began to fall away, shrinking until the sky and a sprinkling of dim stars were again visible. The terrain on the east became a pie-up of massive boulders and tangled brush, while, close to the road edge, fringes of pine made ragged black patches against the backdrop of darkening grey.

O'Grady thumbed tobacco and papers from a shirt pocket and thoughtfully began building a smoke.

He was running his tongue along the paper when an indecipherable curse exploded from up on the box and the stage began braking.

The little man across from him stuck his head out the window, jerking it quickly back when a gun went off.

'It – it's a holdup!'

The third passenger, too busy stuffing a purse into the top of a boot, offered nothing.

O'Grady sat without moving, listening as the driver was made to get rid of his weapons.

'You're wastin' your time, boys,' he was saying to whoever was out there. 'Only thing I'm carryin' is passengers an' some mail. See for yourselves. Ain't even a guard ridin' with me.'

'This's no hold-up. Just everybody stay put and nobody gets hurt.' The voice outside lifted sharply. 'Grady! Step out!'

The man who so far had done the only talking, flung a nervous, questioning look at the passenger beside him. Receiving a slow shake of the head, his eyes swung back to the one opposite. then it was as if he was trying to press deeper into his seat.

O'Grady let loose a silent sigh, ditched the half-made cigarette, and unlatched the door.

'Hands where we can see them,' the voice giving the orders warned.

The hard-packed earth under O'Grady's feet felt a little unsteady when he stepped from the coach, raising his hands to shoulder height. Too long he'd been sitting: first on a train from Canon City to Gunnison, then riding stages as he made his way homeward.

A rider was positioned on either side of the coach,

one with a gun pointing at the driver, the other covering the remaining passengers. A third, stocky and slightly bulging at the belt-line, sat his bay mare closer, weapon levelled at O'Grady. All had neckerchiefs masking their features, holsters belted around linen dusters.

'He got a bag?'

'Up here,' grunted the driver.

'Toss it down, then get rolling.'

Only when the sound of hooves and wheels told of distance did the fourth man ride out from the protective shadows of the trees. He was dressed the same as the others, but in his case the long coat did nothing to conceal his size. On his feet he'd stand as tall as O'Grady, but considerably wider.

Which was probably why he'd stayed hidden until now. In almost identical outfits identification of the others might have been difficult, but the driver, pehaps even one of the passengers, might easily have recognized his proportions.

'Check to see if he's got anything tucked away.' His voice was like boot leather on gravel.

The man nearest dismounted, thick torso more evident as he came over to make the search. 'Clean,' he flung back, finding no hidden weapon.

'Taken up a new line of work, Tavener?' O'Grady asked quietly.

The man before him barely hesitated. Pin-points of fire flashed in his eyes, then the back of his free hand was cutting hard across O'Grady's face.

The fourth man walked his horse in still closer. 'Think you could sneak in without me knowing it, did you?'

Eyes smarting from the blow taken, O'Grady made no reply.

'Nothing gets by me, boy,' the big man went on. 'Hardly was you on that stage when I got the word.' He cleared his throat, spat at the road. 'Moment they turned you loose I had someone watching, reporting back to me.'

'What's it you want, McQuade?'

Hammond McQuade pulled down the neckerchief, exposing a face big and square, with grey eyebrows nearly as thick as the brush-like moustache under his beaked nose.

'Tell you what I don't want. And that's to have a stinking killer, a goddamn jailbird, think he can come sailing back free and easy.'

'Free,' O'Grady returned coldly. 'But not easy. And I am back.'

McQuade's head shook, slowly, emphatically.

'Not by a long way.'

Now the one on foot slipped down his mask. It was someone O'Grady had disliked from the moment of their first encounter: Mel Tavener, ramrod for McQuade's Slash M outfit. Things had happened since then to make him dislike the man even more.

'Royal,' Tavener snapped, and one of the other riders moved over to where they stood. He too had dropped his bandanna to show a narrow face, eyes sunk deep in their sockets. He looked like someone with a sickness gnawing away at his gut.

Tavener sheathed his gun. 'Let's have the rope.'

The man called Royal loosened the lariat from his saddle and casually shook out a loop.

Another racking sound came from McQuade's throat. 'I'm a fair man, O'Grady, but you owe me a lot more'n your miserable life's worth.'

'Got that the wrong way around, haven't you?'

Tavener's hand lashed out again. 'Any more lip,

bucko, and next time it'll be something harder.'

Without expression, Royal nudged his horse forward, flicked his wrist, and let the rope drop over O'Grady's head and settle on his shoulders.

McQuade continued as if there'd been no interruption.

'I'm giving you a chance, one you don't deserve, not after what you done to my boy. Pick up your gear and start walking back the way you came, making sure I never again see your face.' Shifting his eyes to Royal, he gave a curt nod.

The noose lifted, began biting into O'Grady's neck, as the thin rider slowly took up the slack.

'Or,' McQuade's voice rasped through his teeth, 'you get what that damn court should've given you.'

The man who so far had stayed in the rear rode up to McQuade's side. His face remained covered. Which would probably make him Herb Raiker, an ever cautious man, seldom making a play until sure that the odds were in his favour.

McQuade's huge head canted.

'What's it to be?'

'Go to hell,' O'Grady flung back, making no attempt to touch the rope.

'All right,' McQuade motioned brusquely toward Royal. 'You know what to do.'

Tavener stood grinning tightly.

'Watching you kick's going to be a long-awaited pleasure.'

The sick-looking rider tugged on the rope. As he was pulled forward O'Grady grabbed at it, bracing his legs, jerking hard. Almost hauled from leather, Royal let the still coiled length of the lariat fall.

Mel Tavener snatched at his holster, but the shot that followed came from somewhere among the rocks at their rear. McQuade's horse whinnied and reared back, kicking dust and bumping into the horse at its side.

'Another move,' a voice echoed loudly from deep in the gloom, 'and the next one goes higher!'

Tavener's head was swivelling, trying to locate the source of the shot. McQuade got his fiddling mount under control, then he too was scanning the rocks. Nobody, though, made any reckless move.

O'Grady got rid of the rope circling his neck and moved toward Tavener, who was no longer grinning.

He tried to back away, but another rifle shot, this one sailing close above McQuade's head, brought him up short. O'Grady lifted the gun from Tavener's holster, pointing it at the group while placing some extra space between himself and them.

'The rest of you,' the hidden rifleman shouted, 'unload!'

McQuade uttered a rumbling curse, but was the first to empty his holster. Royal, deep-set eyes drilling into O'Grady, was the last to obey.

O'Grady motioned with Tavener's Colt. 'Now the saddle guns.'

Looking up at the dark spaces between the rocks, McQuade's grating voice bellowed, 'You up there! What makes any of this your business? Who the hell are you?'

'Someone who's promised to put a slug into you less'n you do like you're told.'

Silently cursing for having been trapped in such a position, Ham McQuade slid the Winchester from its scabbard, angrily flinging it away. The rest followed his example. Except Tavener, who was on foot.

'Now,' the voice from the rocks ordered, 'turn and ride like hell. Try comin' back, and Tailgate'll have itself a sizeable burying party.'

McQuade glowered down at O'Grady.

'You been warned. You know what's good for you, stay hell and gone out of the county.'

'Better be moving. The gent back there may not be long on patience.'

McQuade's lips started to shape a retort then his mouth clamped shut and he jerked on the reins, swinging his horse away. Like the others his men were using, it showed no brand.

Mel Tavener started for his mount, but O'Grady's voice stopped him halfway there.

'Leave it. You cost me a ride, now you ride back double.'

When they were out of sight, O'Grady turned toward the rocks. With Tavener's gun wedged down behind his belt, he held the reins of the bay left behind, listening to the fading echo of hoofbeats. Waiting.

Shortly, from between the massive boulders and brush, a shod hoof clinked softly upon stone, then, from among the deep shadows a horseman began to materialize.

Alhough the moonlight was pale it was still enough to see the careless grin one rider was wearing.

'I'll be damned!' O'Grady whispered.

3

'Strikes me you already are.' Still smiling, the rider came up to where O'Grady waited. 'Leastways, by ol' Ham.' He leaned down, stretching out a hand of greeting. 'Good seeing you again, Con.'

Slowly shaking his head, O'Grady took the hand offered.

'Josh, it may not be the handsomest, but it's been a while since I've seen a friendlier face.'

Josh Allenby laughed quietly. Seven years younger and a couple of inches shorter than O'Grady, he was sturdily built, with curly black hair and the kind of features that had put a gleam in the eyes of more than one female.

'Light's not good, but you still look as if you'll do.' A frown swiftly killed the grin. 'Rough?'

O'Grady shrugged and nodded toward the rocks. 'Just happen to be camped up there?'

'Blame it on chance. Was still out working when I seen those four cutting across my place. Made me nosy enough to kinda tag along behind.' Josh leaned forward, folding both hands over the saddle horn. 'Looked like they were fixing to hit the stage, so I got myself tucked away, and watched. But when finally the stage comes,' he grinned, 'what's it they want?

21

Why, nothing more valuable than your hide.'

'For which I owe you.'

'Hah!' Josh snorted. 'You've hauled me out of a tight spot or two. 'Sides, McQuade's not stupid. I don't see him trying anything so dumb as a private lynching. Sure, he's been blowing hard, saying if you knew what was good for you, you'd stay well clear of Tailgate. But I figure he was just running a sandy, hoping you'd tuck tail and skedaddle.'

O'Grady's eyes narrowed slightly.

'Only boarded the stage this morning. How could he have found out so fast?'

'Lots of changes since you been away *amigo*. We even got ourselves a real live telegraph line now. If he had someone treadin' on your shadow he could've got word you were on your way, real quick.'

'Lots of changes, Josh?'

It was the younger man's turn to shrug.

'Some.' His gaze shifted to the discarded weapons. 'Best we stash them somewhere, then make tracks.'

When the guns had been collected and dropped behind one of the boulders, O'Grady tied his bag to the saddle of Tavener's mare, and mounted.

'We'll get you another,' Josh promised. 'Send that one on his way back home, 'fore Tavener gets it in his thick skull to claim you stole it.'

'If he did, he'd have some explaining to do.' O'Grady shook his head. 'Tomorrow will be good enough.'

Josh lifted an eyebrow.

'Wouldn't recommend heading out direct for Shamrock, if that's what you got in mind. No telling what that bunch could still try.' He climbed aboard his own mount. 'Tonight you're staying over at my place.'

'Arnie may have something to say about that. Maybe also your father.'

'Not likely. Pa died just six months ago. Double A got split between my half-brother and me. I got the north section, the old house and buildings. Maybe 'cause he's fixing to get married, Arnie drew the long straw; got the new place Pa built, and half the stock.' He laughed, nudging his horse forward. 'Got my own brand now. The JA-Connected. Not bad for a chucked-away kid, huh?'

Not until they were on one of the narrow off-trails that would take them down into Beato Basin was there any more talk, and it was O'Grady who made it.

'Josh, I don't want you having to take on any trouble I may have coming.'

'Meaning?'

'McQuade finds out it was you throwing lead at him . . . .'

' 'Less you tell him, he won't. And you got no reason for doing that.' Josh laughed a little nervously. 'Been wondering just what might've happened had they started shooting back. Hell, I never yet had occasion to wilfully put a bullet in a man.'

They were well into the basin, and because so far there'd been but the one mention of Shamrock, O'Grady voiced the question uppermost in his mind.

Josh reined to a stop.

'Like I said, there's been some changes. Your old crew pulled out.'

'But not Becker.'

'Way I got it,' Josh said, drawing a long breath, 'Tim was the first to go, and without so much as a fare-thee-well.'

In O'Grady's chest there was a slow tightening.

Becker had been his *segundo* – a good man he'd
counted on to hold things together until he
returned.

'It's just guessing,' Josh went on quietly, 'but with
Becker gone it would've been a lot easier for
McQuade to – persuade the rest to quit. He's gotten
to be something of a power of late; took over most of
the small spreads, built up Slash 'til it's now stretched
right down into the basin. He's thrown his weight
around since then and he's got the likes of Tavener
and that Royal Janner to back him.'

O'Grady was silent. When he'd been sent to the
territorial penitentiary for allegedly killing
McQuade's son, Arthur Allenby's had been the
largest of the basin ranches. But his death and the
cutting up of the Double A had evidently changed all
that.

They started moving again, Josh taking the lead,
riding steadily, swinging in a westerly direction.
O'Grady was trying to see the Tim Becker he knew
wouldn't come together. Tim had been a fighter who
believed in loyalty to the brand; if he'd run, someone
must have given him mighty good reason.

'How about your crew?' he queried when lights
from buildings began glimmering through the dark.
'They see us riding in together there could be questions, talk that could reach McQuade.'

'Not likely. None of them've got any love for that
bunch. They're good men; Pa's old hands who chose
to come with me when the ranch got divvied up.'

Light wasn't the only thing coming through the
open bunkhouse windows: to the accompaniment of
a loudly strummed guitar, someone with a slightly
off-key voice was putting all of his heart into the most
mournful of ditties. Josh stopped at the house. He

told O'Grady to go on in, while he'd tend to the horses and let his men know he was back.

Inside the house, O'Grady dumped his bag and lit the lamp. He looked around, remembering when all the Allenbys had lived here: old Arthur, his wife, Arnold their only child and later, Josh.

Then May Allenby had died, and having no wish to continue living where so much of their lives had been spent together, Arthur had decided to build again.

Some of the furniture was old, other bits new, but surprisingly everything was clean and reasonably tidy. Josh had never been very domesticated: Arnie had been the neat, meticulous one. He'd taken after his mother, which was maybe what had made him a little soft, not easily given to the hard work of ranching to which Josh had so quickly adapted. Apparently, becoming the owner of property had provided Josh with a new perspective.

O'Grady stretched out in one of the big chairs and began rolling a cigarette. He'd never been told the entire story, had never been all that interested. Bits and pieces, though, had been picked up, a story of Allenby finding a bundled-up toddler in a liquor-crate left in an alley siding a Denver saloon.

The Allenby's had one child, wanted another, and couldn't. So the kid was brought to the Double A and given the Allenby name. How it was arranged, O'Grady had never made any attempt to find out. When it happened he'd been too young to care, writing it off as he grew older as being none of his business.

Arnie, already two years old, as the gossip told it, had welcomed the novelty of a baby brother. But as they grew, differences began to emerge. Arnie tried to dominate, and Josh wouldn't take it. Fights were regular occurrences, and most of the time it was the older of the pair who came off second best.

O'Grady lit the cigarette, blew smoke at the worn floor rug, wondering if that had been the reason for Arthur Allenby's decision to split the Double A between the two boys rather than have them run it as equal partners. And then he was thinking of his own kid brother . . . .

Perhaps because he had been left largely to fend for themselves while still youngsters, there'd been a strong bond between him and Gil. Shamrock hadn't been much to brag about when their parents died: a vast stretch of prime grazing land with water enough to carry them through dry spells, but still with a herd of no significance.

Together he and Gil had put their backs into it, often doing the work of four men, scrimping and saving every spare dollar, both knowing what they wanted and determined to achieve it.

Memory pulled O'Grady's mouth into a thin smile. They'd still been a long way from their goal that morning Gil came charging up to where he was repairing a fence, yelling as if a bunch of Indians had designs on his scalp.

The sound of the door opening shattered his reverie.

Josh tramped into the house, tossed his hat on to a wall hook, and started peeling off his coat.

'You said Arnie's intending to get married,' O'Grady frowned. 'Local girl?'

In the process of unbuckling his shellbelt, Josh paused. It was a long moment before he answered.

'Uh-huh,' he muttered. 'Stacey Prentice.'

4

Only mildly surprised, O'Grady studied the ash on his cigarette. At another time the news might have stung: now it no longer mattered. He felt nothing. Whatever he and Stacey Prentice once shared had died the night he was accused of killing Lance McQuade.

He'd known that for sure while sitting in a jail cell, waiting to be transported to prison. If Stacey had wanted to see him, she'd have come, regardless of Dan Prentice's advice to stay away.

He stood up, killed the cigarette in an earthen bowl where two other butts lay crushed.

'See what you meant about changes.'

'Yeah,' Josh nodded. 'Surprised me, too.'

'Things happen,' O'Grady said impassively. 'How about Box D? How's it doing?'

'Walt's OK, but old Maddy's not too good. Had a – a stroke, I think the doc called it. Talks a little funny now. Needs a stick to get around.'

From a cabinet O'Grady remembered as once being the storage place for May Allenby's best crockery, Josh fetched a bottle and glasses. He poured until both glasses were half-filled.

'Cookie'll be bringing along some grub,' he said,

27

handing one of the drinks to O'Grady, raising his own.

'Meanwhile – to old times, and better times ahead.'

Motioning O'Grady back to his seat, he took a place on the couch.

'OK to ask a personal question?'

'Go ahead.'

In decent light Josh was getting his first clear look at the man opposite him, and what he saw made him put a hold on the question. Two years of prison toil had wrought changes. O'Grady had lost some weight, his face looked a little gaunt, and the somewhat stern expression seemed to have sunk in a little deeper. Thick, brown hair showed a powdering of grey at the temples, and in those dark eyes lurked something hard and impenetrable.

'Now you're back . . . is it your plan to stay? Or maybe get rid of Shamrock, and clear out?'

'Why? Thinking of adding to your holdings?'

'Hell, no. Was askin', is all.'

Josh took another pull at his drink, relaxed against the couch's backrest.

'Glad to hear that.'

'Why'd you ask, Josh?'

'Told you, McQuade's become a power, and he's getting greedy. He's had his eye on your place for a time, and if ever he was to get his claws on it, he'd have the rest of us boxed in.'

O'Grady listened, but he was thinking about the letters the bank had written. 'If ever he succeeds, it won't be because I sold. Besides, I've got another reason for staying.'

Josh's forehead creased faintly.

'Gil,' O'Grady reminded. 'My brother.'

'Yeah.' Josh nodded. 'I'd near forgot.'

'I haven't.' O'Grady swallowed on the rest of his drink. *Or that, although he'd never had a chance to prove it, it was Lance McQuade who'd put those two bullets in Gil's back.*

Josh looked down into his glass, nodding almost imperceptibly.

'Yeah Prentice was sure as hell quick to lock you up, but he's still not done much about finding your brother's killer.' His gaze lifted. 'Con, I never doubted you when you said you didn't kill McQuade's pup.'

O'Grady put down the empty glass.

'I didn't. It was an accident, exactly as I told it in court.'

'Which brings us to Arnie.'

'Why? He only told what he saw when he came into the Ten Spot. Trouble was, he got there too late and never saw all of it.'

Josh let out his breath, reached for the bottle. 'That oughta give him ease. He's been doing some sweating about how you'd feel, him having testified against you.'

In silence O'Grady watched him tilt the bottle. It had been a while since he'd talked this much, or tasted whiskey, good or otherwise.

Next morning, his duffel transferred to borrowed saddle-bags, O'Grady was pointed south, holding down an urge to head directly for Shamrock, to find out what had happened in his absence. First, though, he needed to make a call at the bank and settle a few things still weighing heavily on his mind.

Then, with Allenby land behind him, he thought, the hell with it; another hour or two wasn't going to make any difference.

Swinging off the stage road, he cut a trail easterly, travelling deeper into the basin, riding without haste, picking up old landmarks, finally coming to a stop where Glidden wire was strung across the notch between low but steep-sided hills.

A slightly sad smile tugged at his mouth. This was the drift fence he'd been repairing the morning Gil came racing up to where he worked, yelling as if he were under attack. But after Gil'd calmed down enough to speak, he'd dropped his tools, and together they'd taken off, back in the direction from which Gil had come.

It wasn't big, the pocket of silver Gil had stumbled upon, petering out completely after just a couple of months' working. But its yield was enough to settle everything with the bank, pay off patient merchants, and still leave something over. It was then that Shamrock began to rise proud. Not the biggest in the basin, but surely one of the best.

In another moment the smile was gone and there was a tightening to his jaws as he gazed aong the length of the fence to where wire sagged and posts leaned at drunken angles. Almost dead centre was a gap wide enough through which to drive a wagon.

He swore softly, got Tavener's mare moving and headed through the gap.

They must have been watching, the two who suddenly appeared from the small grove of trees not a half-mile beyond the hills. They rode out without haste, crossing his path, waiting for him.

One was jowled, thick-lipped, and unshaven, greasy Levis encasing thick thighs. His eyes narrowed as O'Grady drew up in front of him, trying to find an identifying brand on the bay horse.

'Just where the hell you figure you're going?'

O'Grady jerked a thumb to his right.

'Tailgate that way?'

'So?'

'Then you got the answer to your question.'

'Snooty bastard,' the second, a sharp-featured lightweight, sneered.

The heavier man's head canted to the left. 'You riding for Allenby?'

'No.' O'Grady lifted the reins, made as if to swing around them. 'And if you've no more questions, I'll be moving on.'

The smaller of the pair stepped his mount quickly forward, blocking the path.

'Not this way you ain't. This's Shamrock you're on. Which means you're trespassin'.'

Ignoring him, O'Grady turned to his partner. 'You the rangeboss?'

Intead of answering, almost lazily the man's right hand dropped, rising again to point the Colt he had lifted from leather.

'Why? You 'bout to give us some argument?'

O'Grady shrugged.

'Too pleasant a day for any of that.' He started to turn the horse under him, then paused. 'Case you hadn't noticed, you've got a broken fence back there.'

A shot blasted asunder the morning stillness, causing the bay to rear back. A second shot only just missed putting a rip in the shoulder of O'Grady's deerskin jacket.

'You're dawdlin',' the smaller one snarled, whipping out his own gun.

Swinging the skittish mount around, O'Grady started back the way he'd come, keeping a lid on an anger fast on the boil. Allowing himself to be driven off the land where so much of his life had been spent was a galling thing. Behind his belt was shoved Mel Tavener's gun, but he let it stay there, refusing to give the horse its head when still more lead raked the air.

At its birth it had been given a different name, one that had received little use. For reasons obscured by time and memory, someone had chosen to put up a sign ... using the tailgate of a junked freighter to accommodate the required lettering.

Then, no sooner had the town, now being called Tailgate, started to grow when newly arrived settlers and merchants began pointing out the advantages of relocating closer to the creek.

O'Grady took his eyes away from the distant grey smudge of deserted and dilapidated buildings now referred to simply as Old Town, and gazed down upon those sprawled along the other side of Tower Creek's slow-moving waters. He remembered how it had been the day he'd left.

It was no coincidence that the clothes he wore now were almost exactly the same as the ones he'd been wearing when, with half the town's population turned out to watch, he'd been loaded aboard the stage. That day, though, he'd also worn leg-irons and manacles.

He started the bay down toward the bridge, pulling over to the side of the road when seeing a buggy approaching from the opposite direction.

Fingers lifted automatically to the brim of his hat when the vehicle drew abreast of where he waited. The dark-haired girl who held the reins responded with a nod and a brief smile, leaving him twisted on the saddle, watching the roll of dust long after the buggy had disappeared over the rise.

5

Not much in Tailgate had changed, yet everything seemed somehow different, older and smaller than he remembered. Like something left too long to bake in the sun.

Few on the sidewalks wasted so much as a glance his way as he rode down the wide, dusty street, passing the hardware store, saddle shop, Mossman's General Emporium, which occupied a block of its own, Hannah's Café and other places he'd once frequented. He halted briefly when reaching the Ten Spot.

Here was where it had cost him two years of his life.

After the meeting of cattlemen broke up he'd stayed in town, killing time until Amy Brewster eventually emerged from Mossman's, apprehension paling her face when finding him waiting for her. It had taken some persuasion before she'd permitted him to escort her home, still more to get her to talk.

A week past, Gil had gone into town to pick up supplies. He'd been late starting off, so no one was particularly concerned when, long after dark, he'd still not returned. Next morning, one of the crew sent to find out what was keeping him, found the loaded buckboard and team pulled off the road, Gil with two bullet holes in his back.

They'd buried him, waited for the law to find his killer, and when it hadn't, O'Grady had taken it upon himself to check Gil's backtrail.

He'd felt just a little hurt having to learn from others that a couple of times his younger brother had been seen taking home a girl who worked at Mossman's Emporium. For reasons he would never know, Gil hadn't once mentioned her.

A good while later, after leaving the tiny cabin in which Amy Brewster lived, he'd walked back the few blocks to the town centre, uncertain of what to do with what he'd learned. Going to Dan Prentice with no more than a pretty good hunch would be time wasted.

And then he remembered the horses seen in front of the Ten Spot.

It was mid-week, and late, so there were few customers in the saloon. Just Mel Tavener, Red Scheil and Herb Raiker, all riders for Hammond McQuade's Slash M iron. They and the boss man's whelp, already on his way to getting stoned.

O'Grady continued on to the livery barn, turning the bay over to an overweight man he'd never seen before. 'Belongs to Slash,' he told him, removing the borrowed saddle-bags. 'Someone'll be around to pick it up.'

A question began to loom in the other's eyes, but O'Grady got his in first.

'What happened to Phil Sanders?'

'Said he was going to California. Sold out to me. Name's Buchner. Gabe Buchner. Usually got some-one handling things here for me, but—'

'Got something I can hire for a day or two?'

'Right now,' the fat man wheezed regretfully, 'not much. Claybank back there don't look like a whole lot, but he'll take you wherever you got to be.'

A short while later O'Grady was riding the blocky horse back down Tailgate's main street. His name, when he'd given it, had apparently meant little or nothing to Buchner. But that of Shamrock had been sufficient, leaving him to wonder why.

Two years had cost Joe Lennon a little more hair, otherwise he looked much the same, seated there at the teller's window, counting coins into sacks. With little interest he cast a quick glance at the street door when the bell above it jangled, not looking up again until a voice offered a curt greeting and told him what its owner wanted.

A small, lipless man, Lennon stiffened, sliding quickly off the high stool, head bobbing eagerly.

It was a while before he returned to hold open the gate in the slatted rail, grabbing nervously at the visitor's arm once he was inside the enclosure.

'Mr O'Grady, I had no wish to be on that jury. I – I swear, it was forced upon me.'

'Sure,' O'Grady muttered, and crossed to the office built into the corner of the room.

A bespectacled Terry Washburn came around the desk, hand outstretched, smiling.

O'Grady returned the moist hand, glad to let it go.

'It was your father I wanted to see.'

Washburn went back to his place behind the desk, waving his visitor into one of two high-backed chairs.

'Dad's retired. Developed a heart problem.'

From his coat pocket O'Grady took two letters and unfolded them. Both were signed T. Washburn.

Mistakenly, he'd assumed the initial to stand for Thomas, the Bank's founder.

Considerably shorter than his father, Terry Rashburn was already running to fat. Perhaps in an effort to make himself look either older or more businesslike, he'd cultivated a thin blond moustache. He gave each of the letters handed to him a quick scan, then put them aside. Before he could say anything, O'Grady asked:

'W–who was it made the offer?'

Lacing his fingers together, Washburn leaned back in the leather swivel chair.

'Since you declined to sell, I'm afraid I'm not at liberty to say.'

'Ham McQuade?'

A shadow passed quickly over Washburn's round face.

'As I've told you . . . I'm not free to say.'

O'Grady nodded.

'McQuade.'

'What if it was?' Behind rimless glasses the banker's eyes grew small. 'It may still be in your best interests to sell. Were you to do so, I'm quite sure I could find you a very fair offer.'

'You figure McQuade's was fair?'

'Under the circumstances—'

'It was an insult,' O'Grady growled quietly.

'I – I could try to talk to him.'

'Thanks, but I'd sooner we looked at the books.'

Washburn shut his mouth and went to the safe, returning with two books, one small and blue, the other a thick journal, which he placed in front of O'Grady before resuming his seat.

'Every transaction has been faithfully recorded, just as you'd been doing.'

The journal was O'Grady's own, turned over to the bank when placing his financial affairs in the hands of Washburn's father.

'Something wrong?' Washburn queried noticing the tightening of his client's jaw while looking through a section of the book.

'Tim Becker was instructed to make a gather of around a hundred, to sell them at the nearest shipping point. Don't see anything about it here.'

'That's because it was never done.'

More was coming and O'Grady waited for it. He found the makings, began building a cigarette.

'For a while there was quite a spate of rustling in the basin. Shamrock, unfortunately, was worst hit. Then your man Becker chose to up and leave. One of the others tried to hire temporary hands, to make the drive, but couldn't find anyone who'd sign on.' Pale hands made a gesture to emphasize the rest. 'It was a difficult time.'

'Must've been,' O'Grady said tightly. 'Even the calf crop is too damned low to be natural.'

Washburn shrugged. 'Those are the figures given to me by your foreman.'

'Why'd my original crew quit?'

'I've no idea, though Becker's sudden decision to seek greener pastures may have had something to do with it. Whichever, I daresay they had their reasons.'

'Yeah,' O'Grady grunted, 'I daresay.' He got the cigarette burning, dropped the match into an ashtray that looked as if it had never been used.

'Naturally,' Washburn went on, 'when the other two rode in, asking for the pay they had coming, I tried to find out. However, they'd give no reason for electing to leave.'

O'Grady flipped pages until coming to the section

of the journal where expenses were recorded.

Washburn produced a snow-white handkerchief and began polishing his glasses, all the while watching the long forefinger running down the entries.

Abruptly O'Grady killed his smoke and shut the book.

'What gives, Terry? Expenses have never been this high, not in the history of Shamrock.'

Washburn fitted the spectacles back into position.

'I think we ought to understand something. When you were . . . forced to leave, you asked the bank to manage your finances, not to control or run your operation. Questions concerning expenses ought to be taken up with your present foreman.'

'Who is?'

'His name is Alda. Fred Alda. And as for the expenses, I can assure you, at the time they were incurred, each appeared perfectly justified.'

'Who hired this new crew?'

'Why . . . I did. It needed to be done if the ranch was to continue functioning.'

'On someone's recommendation?'

'No. I simply put out the word.'

O'Grady's mouth twisted into a thin smile that was reflected nowhere else. 'Must've been quite a change of heart around here, considering no one was interested in hiring on before then.'

'I sincerely hope that's not intended to imply something.' Washburn tried to sound offended.

Instead of answering, O'Grady said, 'Let's get to the bottom line, Terry. What kind of money do I have left?'

'Not much, I'm sorry to say.' The blue passbook was slid across the desk, and so that he'd not have to meet the other's gaze, Washburn busied himself carefully refolding his handkerchief.

Not much was right. Shamrock should have earned enough to carry not only the operating costs, but also to produce a profit. Instead, according to the records, though there'd been no shipments, the size of his herd had actually shrunk and his operating capital run down to virtually nothing. The bank book showed a balance of just slightly over $300. O'Grady pushed up out of the chair.

'Anybody still owed anything?'

'No . . .'

Relief lifted some of the stiffness from O'Grady's shoulders.

'Then I'll manage.'

In his pocket was eighteen dollars, the last of a small sum held by the warden's office, pending his release, and the ten dollars presented to him when finally that day had come.

'One – uh – other thing I believe you should know,' Washburn mumbled, gently dabbing at his mouth with the folded handkerchief. 'The bank has had its own problems. Presently we're in no position to extend any loans or consider new ones.'

O'Grady picked up the journal. 'Now why does that come as no big surprise?'

On the sidewalk he took time to roll another smoke while observing the activity along the street. Legal claims and manipulations the kind he could not have foreseen, were what had concerned him most. They were what could have jeopardized everything he and Gil had worked for.

As it was, while imprisoned, he'd been systematically robbed. A blind man going over the records would have spotted what was happening. So how come Washburn hadn't?

He thought he might know the answer to that one.

McQuade wanted Shamrock, and, according to Josh Allenby he'd become something of a power in the past two years. Perhaps even powerful enough to exert pressure on the bank.

He was buckling the saddle-bag into which he'd dropped the journal when they pulled up close behind him. Slowly he turned around.

Flanked by the skinny Royal Janner and a heavy mule-faced man, Mel Tavener sat sneering down at him.

'Don't hear too well, does he?' Janner said.

'Seems not.' Tavener leaned forward in his saddle. 'Who was your friend hidden in them rocks?'

'Ever you find out,' O'Grady returned, 'be sure and let me know. Like to tell him thanks.' He started turning back to the hitch rack, and stopped. 'You'll find your mare at the livery. Also your gun. The rest are among those rocks you were talking about.'

Tavener's back straightened, his face hardening.

Leather creaked loudly when the rider at his left swung heavily to the ground, a small grin of anticipation on his mulish face.

'You deaf, jailbird? Mel asked you something.'

'And I'll tell you what was intended for him. Go to hell.'

A block of a man with pale, rust-coloured hair, Scheil's nose had been broken enough times to turn it into a shapeless lump. The story was he'd once been a ring fighter, though most knew him only as another of Slash M's bucko boys. His grin stretched wider.

'Now that's the talk I like to hear.'

Hardly had he spoken when a fist the size of a mallet was sailing towards O'Grady's face.

6

O'Grady saw the fist coming with Scheil's bulk piled
up behind it. He stepped quickly to the side, clasping
both hands together as he moved. He lifted them
high, and when Scheil, missing his target, lurched on
by, brought them down with battering-ram force,
right elbow driving into his attacker's ribs.

A pained gasp erupted from Scheil's throat, but
momentum kept him going until the tie-rail got in
his way. Just when it seemed sure he'd continue over
the top, he managed to jerk back, lost his balance,
and raised a small cloud of dust when coming down
hard on his broad rump.

A sense of satisfaction surged through O'Grady.
He'd come out leaner, but two years of imprisonment had hardened him, taught him how to take
care of himself among strong men a whole lot
tougher than Red Scheil might ever hope to be.

He faced Tavener. 'Any more questions?'

Tavener ignored him, eyes on Scheil climbing
awkwardly to his feet, wincing sharply when fully
erect. Sucking in a huge lungful of air, he muttered
a low curse and readied himself for another attack.

'That's it!' Tavener snapped, while, at his side
some personal amusement had Royal Janner smiling.

Scheil paused, an expression of stupidity on his long face. 'Damnit, Mel!' Hate-filled eyes returned to O'Grady. 'The son of a bitch ain't getting away wih that!'

'There'll be another time,' Tavener promised tightly. 'Mount up.'

'You're dead,' Scheil snarled, stumbling back to his horse. 'You hear me? Next time you're dead!'

Puzzled as to why Tavener had ordered Scheil to quit, O'Grady watched them ride off. He got his answer when a mild and familiar voice said:

'Didn't take you long to find trouble, did it?'

He came around to see an unsmiling Dan Prentice poised on the edge of the sidewalk.

'Maybe it found me.'

'I miss something?'

'Not much,' O'Grady answered quietly, a little shaken by the changes a couple of years had wrought in the man before him. Of only medium height Prentice had always been on the slender side. Now he was as thin as a whistle, a slump in his narrow shoulders.

As if dismissing the subject, Prentice nodded. 'Been wondering when you'd show.'

'When or if, Dan?'

'Little of both, I guess.'

In uncomfortable silence the two regarded each other, each wanting to say something more, neither prepared to be the first. There'd been a time when they'd been close friends, when Dan Prentice had looked forward to the day Conner O'Grady and his niece would tie the knot. But a saloon fight had changed all that.

O'Grady said, 'Was on my way to see you.'

'Figured you'd be.' Prentice started walking away.

'Let's take it up elsewhere.'

In the sheriff's office he stopped at the side of his desk. 'Stage driver reported what happened. I rode out to where he said he'd been stopped. Found hoof-prints a-plenty, but no trail that could be followed.' He picked up a short-stemmed pipe from a clay ashtray. 'What happened?'

'Maybe you'd better ask Ham McQuade.'

Watery blue eyes narrowed. 'What are you trying to tell me?'

'Forget it. The last time I tried telling people here the truth there wasn't anyone who'd listen.' O'Grady shuttled a fast glance around the room. It looked almost exactly as it had the last time he'd seen it. 'Anything been done about Gil's death?'

A deep sigh dragged Prentice's shoulders down a little more. 'Aiming to stir up more trouble?'

'Like I thought,' O'Grady said. 'Nothing.'

Between his fingers the match Prentice was about to strike snapped in two. He flung it to the floor. 'Don't you stand there and tell me that! I've got nowhere because there were no leads then and none've turned up since.' His gaze dropped to the unlit pipe he was holding. 'I've been running this office for years without any damned help, and only because this town's too stinking tight to pay wages for more than a temporary deputy. But that don't mean I haven't done what's needed doing!'

'Nobody has to tell me that, Dan. You took me in when you had to.'

Prentice got rid of the pipe. 'It's over, Con. You're a free man again. Let it lie.'

'Not so easy. It cost me two years because someone like McQuade was big enough to have people rig evidence and lie for him.'

Another sigh slipped across Prentice's lips. 'Still insisting his boy was packing a gun?'

'Let me ask you a question, Dan. Same one I asked back then. You ever see him without that fancy rig he had made for himself?'

'Maybe not. But how come nobody else saw it that night?'

'They saw it, including the bartender. Hell, he was scared spitless when he gave testimony. He was lying through his teeth; he knew that while I was out cold Tavener or one of those with him, got rid of it. Same thing with the bottle he stepped on.'

'Again, why? What'd be the point?'

'I don't know, not for sure. But I've had lots of time to think. Tavener's always hated my guts. That was a way for him to really get at me. It also made a better story to hand his boss, better than having to tell him his son died like a drunken idiot. Better than having him know the boy was a yellow-streaked back-shooter.'

'Damnit, Con, you've no proof of that. All the girl told you was that Lance was sore as a boil 'cause she'd turned him down in favour of Gil.'

'And that he went to her place drunk, tried to force his way in. Only he hadn't figured on Gil being there, or that he'd get the hell knocked out of him. And that was probably what earned Gil two slugs in the back.'

'You're still guessing. There's no way to—'

'I'll prove it, Dan. Hell and high water, I'll see Gil's killer branded for what he was. And this time, if trouble comes my way, I won't let myself be suckered like before.' He took a tug at his hat brim, said, 'See you around,' and started for the door. Then, remembering something, stopped and made a half-turn. 'So far

I've been to only the livery barn and the bank, but at neither place were there any questions about me being taken off that stage.'

'Maybe they thought better than to mention it. Right now you don't look like the most approachable person around.'

O'Grady nodded, but before he could move Prentice said, 'You haven't asked about Stacey.'

'Thought you'd prefer it that way. It was you who kept her from seeing me, remember?'

'It's what I thought was best for her. Getting yourself in that mess, it . . . .' Prentice whipped off his hat, scraped fingers through thinning grey hair, and avoided looking at O'Grady. 'I was protecting her, that's all, doing what I thought was best.'

And it built a wall between you and me, Dan, the kind we may never be able to knock down.

'She's set to get married,' Prentice went on, voice down as he lifted his gaze. 'To Arnie Allenby.'

'Congratulate them for me,' O'Grady murmured, and went out into the midday sun.

The Denton's Box D was a good-sized outfit, situated on the bend of Crocker's Creek, west of Shamrock. The long rambling house was constructed of pine logs, as were most of the other buildings, with pole corrals sited north of the barn and blacksmith shop.

They'd had three children, the Dentons, of whom only Walt, the first born, still lived. Accidents had taken both the younger ones. And, while still a comparatively young man, Dave, Maddy's husband, had cashed in during a bout with pneumonia.

It was Maddy Denton, a good neighbour, who'd taken the O'Grady boys under her wing when their parents had died, becoming like a second mother to them until quite certain they were capable of managing on their own.

Down from the centre corral came the sounds of activity, men's voices, the snorting and stomping of a horse. O'Grady paid it all small attention, more interested in the figure seated in one of the two chairs on the shaded veranda of the house.

With the help of a cane the woman pushed awkwardly up out of the chair when he dismounted, took a step toward the veranda rail, squinting against the light. Her right arm hung limply at her side.

'Conner?'

He wrapped the claybank's reins and went up the wide plank steps. 'Hello, Miss Maddy.'

Sturdy of frame, iron-grey hair cut to manageable length, Maddy Denton's face wore a bunch of new lines. 'Con. It's really you!'

He smiled, removed his hat and went to her.

Still in her embrace, movement at the open front door brought his head up. He looked over Maddy's shoulder and saw someone carrying a wooden tray come through the doorway.

The girl froze, and, standing like that, mouth slightly open, O'Grady thought she looked even lovelier than when he'd seen her driving the buggy out of Tailgate.

7

Her dress was of pale pink gingham, simple in design, yet it did not conceal the graceful moulding of her figure. A thin ribbon held in place shoulder-length hair the colour of burnished gold. Her name was Susan Blayne.

'I–I'll fetch another cup,' she said after Maddy had made the introductions, took her hand out of O'Grady's, and went quickly back into the house.

'Been in Tailgate six months,' Maddy said in reply to his frowned question. 'Works as a teacher, part-time until old Kermit Taylor retires. In between she lends Doc Brophy a hand.'

When she spoke there was a sight slurring of her words, a small drooping at the left of her mouth that deepened the furrows in O'Grady's brow.

Maddy shook her head. 'Don't fret. I'm doing okay, now. Susan just comes out to make sure I stay that way.' She turned, permitting him to help her back to her chair. 'The old grey mare' she said, once comfortable, the stick rested across her legs, 'ain't what she used to be.'

'Things all right here, Miss Maddy?'

'Everything considered, fine, I guess.'

Susan Blayne returned to busy herself at the table

47

where she'd deposited the tray.

'Maddy's often talked about you,' she said, handing him a cup of the coffee she'd poured.

O'Grady's tossed glance at the older woman received a slow nod. 'Susan's more than just a good friend. I've told her how McQuade had you railroaded.'

About to say something, the girl's gaze made a sudden shift, a smile shaping up on her face just as someone at O'Grady's rear said:

'Now if it was me, I'd be sure to let folks know, so's they could roll out the welcome carpet.'

A tall, angular man, somewhere in his early forties, stood at the bottom of the steps, his grin wide, clothes sweated through and caked with dust.

'Wait, you old brush-thumper,' O'Grady smiled, and went to take the hand thrust at him.

The grin gone, Walt Denton stroked his drooping moustache. 'When you're through, I'll be over at the bunkhouse wash-trough, getting cleaned up.'

Back on the veranda, O'Grady found a perch on the rail while Susan Blayne rose from the chair in which she'd seated herself, and refilled his cup. Maddy began telling of developments in the basin, but abruptly, in the middle of a sentence, her mouth clamped shut and she slapped irritably at her thigh.

'Enough of that! I'm making small talk 'cause I don't know how to ask how it was up there.' She looked hard up at him. 'They treat you OK?'

'Let's just say I wouldn't volunteer for another of those vacations.'

A short while later Susan got up to take the tray and its contents back to the kitchen. When she returned she was carrying a small but bulging carpet bag. 'It's time I was starting back,' she announced.

He walked her to where the buggy was parked in front of the barn, and got the horse back into harness.

Buttoning the same soiled shirt, Walt Denton came from around the side of the bunkhouse to say his goodbye, afterwards watching with O'Grady until the buggy was lost to sight. 'Quite a girl, that.'

O'Grady lifted an eyebrow.

Denton laughed and shook his head. 'Not me. Been footloose and fancy-free too long to think of changing. Couldn't help noticing, though, the way you were getting somewhat calf-eyed in her company.'

'You mentioned a need to talk,' O'Grady said gruffly, uncomfortably aware of an unnatural warmth rising into his face.

Loosing another short laugh, Denton led the way back to the house and the room used as an office.

'Been home yet?' he asked once there.

'On my way.'

'Then prepare yourself. It's been allowed to run itself darn near into the ground. Me and a couple of the boys were keeping an eye on the place, but those hardcases the bank brought in didn't take kindly to our intentions. Warned us to stay well clear. Came close to trading lead when it was hinted it was probably us running off Shamrock stock.'

'Talked with Terry Washburn before coming here. He mentioned there'd been some rustling.'

'Some is right,' Denton snorted. 'We lost a few head, so did others. But it'd take the likes of a blind fool not to see that what was going on was aimed mostly at your place.' From pockets in his sweated shirt he produced tobacco and papers. 'Dan Prentice did a lot of riding that turned up nothing. Soon afterwards it stopped. Leastways, we had no more losses. Nor anybody else I know of.'

'Telling me something, Walt?'

Denton sifted tobacco into a curved paper.

'If I am, it's this. Seems to me like someone was trying real hard to either wipe you out or cripple you, and if that's so, it shouldn't be tough guessing who. Hell, I'll give good odds on those three having been installed only so's they could strip your range.' He passed over the makings. 'You're going to have a time getting things back in shape, but you need any help, all you need do is give a holler.'

'Appreciate that,' O'Grady murmured thoughtfully, starting to build himself a smoke. 'Walt, you got any idea why Becket and the others quit?'

'Let me ask you something,' said Denton, taking a while to answer. 'You was a mind to drift, reckon you'd do so leaving behind most of what you owned?'

'You know that for a fact?'

'It's what Turner and Coxe told me. Said most of Tim's stuff was still in the bunkhouse. It's part of what scared them off. They figured him dead, and I kind of go along with that.'

'Prentice check it out?'

'What was to check? The man was gone, that's the only thing any of us knew for certain.'

From a beat-out trunk standing against an inner wall, Denton hauled out a burlap sack that appeared to hold contents of some weight.

'Ma had us board up the house so's nobody could mess with your private stuff, not that I think it's done a whole hell of a lot of good. This, though, I brought over here. Your gun rig's inside. So's Gil's.'

O'Grady took the sack, making no attempt to examine the contents.

'Con, those three supposed to be working your place, they're a mean bunch of bastards. You want, me and a couple of the boys, we'll ride back with you.'

'Thanks, but this I need to take care of myself.'

Denton nodded. 'Then at least let me get you something worth riding. Leave that crowbait here and I'll have it taken back to town.'

For two years he'd thought of little else except to be back where he belonged, but, as a free man again, it was taking him a while getting there. The shadows were already long when finally he rode the borrowed sorrel away from Box D.

A half-hour after fording Crocker's Creek, he drew rein on the downgrade of a low pine-covered hill to look upon the house nestled in the shade of giant cottonwoods.

From the sack Denton had given him he took his gunbelt, buckled it on, and checked the Colt. Packing five of the empty chambers, he contemplated his calloused hands. Once they'd been possessed of reasonable ability; now he wondered just how much of that remained.

Angling across the ranch yard, the first thing to snag his attention were the boards nailed across the door and windows of the house, the little of wind-dumped leaves and dirt piled up on the veranda.

His eyes were on the bunkhouse, at the two saddled horses standing out front, when a figure appeared at the door, spoke something over its shoulder, and moved back out of sight.

He was dismounted and waiting at the tie-rail in front of the house, when three men showed themselves: two he'd met before. The heaviest walked slightly ahead of the others, jowls wobbling as his boots struck hard against the ground.

'Thought I told you to steer clear of this range?' he barked when coming to a halt, the others stopping close behind.

'Not something I need reminding of,' he said tightly, remembering when he'd tried crossing Shamrock on his way to town. At the bank he'd been told the present foreman was a Fred Alda. This would be him. 'Now I've got something for you. Collect your gear, and clear out. All of you.'

'Yeah?' This time it was the lightweight who'd been with Alda who spoke. 'And who the hell're you to give us orders?'

'The name's O'Grady.'

Without batting an eye, Alda hooked thumbs into the front of his belt, an insolent grin peeling back thick lips. 'We supposed to take your word for that?'

'Besides, we're owed pay,' said the lightweight.

'Take it up with the one who hired you.'

Nothing he'd so far said had made a dent in their smug attitudes. Which could mean that someone had prepared them for his arrival. He shot a fast glance at the saddled horses and the third man, who had been partially concealed by Alda's bulk, threw himself sideways, right arm pushing forward so the gun he held was pointed straight at O'Grady's chest.

'Supposing we decide to collect right now?'

Alda was laughing when he and the lightweight drew their own weapons. Damning himself for having been suckered in such a manner, O'Grady waited until they were almost upon him, then lunged, letting fly with a vicious right to Alda's heavy jaw. He heard a grunt when knuckles crunched against skin and bone, and Alda fell back, swung toward the lightweight but was too late to avoid the gun barrel sweeping down at his skull.

While still reeling from the blow, one of them got in from behind, bulldozed him to the ground, and the others piled in, fists and boots smashing into face and body.

When it stopped he was little more than a heaving lump of pain. Then the front of his shirt was being bunched up, his head jerked from the ground. A hand whipped back and forth across his face . . . a voice demanded an answer to a question . . . a voice belonging to Mel Tavener.

There seemed to be only one question that went on endlessly. He heard sounds rasp from his throat, a violent curse explode into his face, and his head was almost torn from his shoulders. But by then a fog hovered over his brain, obliterating pain and reality. Through it drifted the distant echo of voices.

'You're wasting your time. He's out cold.'

Swearing again, Tavener let him drop. The fog began to swirl darkly.

'What do we do now?' It sounded like Alda.

'Drift.' Mel Tavener again, bossing the show.

'Just like that?'

'What the hell're you crying about? You made a chunk out of the beef run off this place.'

'Yeah? Strikes me McQuade didn't do so bad either, what with all those . . . .'

There was more, but the fog had become a whirlpool, sucking him down into its Stygian depth.

8

The dim light was still there when again he opened his eyes. So was the pain. This time, though, he could distinguish things, the oak bureau with its oval mirror, the worn leather chair. He turned his head and discovered the soft glow of a lamp on the table beside the bed on which he lay. He tried to reach it, to turn up the light, but there was a blanket covering him that felt as if it was woven from lead.

Consciousness came and went. Susan Blayne smiled sadly at him while grim-faced, Maddy leaned on a walking stick, scolding him for being a fool and allowing himself to be set up. Lance McQuade pushed them aside, laughing drunkenly when the jurymen delivered their verdict. Very clearly, he heard Judge Emil Sunderson hand down sentence.

'Con? You awake?'

He blinked against the light which had grown brighter, and another voice spoke up gruffly. 'Move aside, boy. Let's have a look at him.' Then someone was bending over the bed, subjecting him to a taste of hell as fingers poked and probed his body.

'How'd I get here?' he croaked, and the first voice he'd heard – Josh Allenby's – replied.

'One of my boys was in town,' he answered from

54

where he hovered close to the background. 'Heard talk that you was back, so I figured I'd ride down and say howdy. Got here and found you out front.'

'And like a sensible lad,' Doc Brophy said in a manner that suggested he did not consider his patient in the same category, 'got you inside, and came to fetch me.' He straightened up, shaking his head. 'No bones broken, but don't nobody ask me why not.'

He stepped back, a small man with a mop of grey hair, and a bulbous nose possessed of a cherry glow. 'See if you can sit up. Got some patching to do.'

With Josh's help, O'Grady sat up and swung his feet to the floor, wondering how much of Allenby's story was true, how much had been fabricated for Brophy's benefit. To let on that he'd known O'Grady was home again would be as good as admitting he'd been around when the stage was stopped.

Only when he was through working did Brophy say, 'All right. Now we talk. How'd this happen?'

'Forget it, Doc. It's done.'

'Tell me, damnit. I'll report it to Prentice.'

'And he'll want proof, which I don't have.'

'Stubborn as ever,' the medico grunted, and put a hand gently on O'Grady's shoulder. 'But still good to have you back. Appears, though, someone else doesn't share the same sentiments.'

'It was them three that were supposed to be taking care of things, wasn't it?' Anger put an edge on Josh's question, making it an accusation.

'Leave it, Josh.'

Brophy eased O'Grady down against the pillows. 'Like I said, mule stubborn.'

Sunlight streaming through the window finally awoke O'Grady. He was stiff, every part of his body ached, but compared to the night before he was wholly alive, his mind clear. He struggled out of bed and got into his clothes.

In the kitchen he found a pot in which Josh had made some kind of stew and, next to the stove, a neat stack of wood. On the table were provisions Josh said he'd taken from the cookshack. He got the fire going, and, while the stew warmed, brewed coffee.

Last night he'd had no appetite; this morning he ate like a man rediscovering food.

The rest of the day was spent lolling on the bed and wandering through the house, opening windows to get rid of the hot, stale air.

In spite of it being boarded up, someone had been in the house. Probably more times than just once. The signs were everywhere; among the books that had been his mother's, in drawers and cupboards, and in the dust that lay like a grey pall over everything.

In the big front room, he stood at the fireplace, studying the carefully selected stones his father had used to build it. He let his gaze drop to the bits of unburned wood poking through the ashes, wondering if they were the remains of the last fire he'd made, or from one more recent.

Legs outstretched, a sullen expression on his face, Mel Tavener sat in McQuade's office, biting back things he knew would shut the buzzard-beaked old bastard up once and for all. But this was not yet the time, and so he sat and listened and said nothing.

'Next time,' McQuade's gravelly voice cut at him, 'you tell me what you've been up to, don't let me have to wait for Prentice to come asking questions that catch me on the left leg.'

'How'd he find out?'

'What the hell made you think he wouldn't? Thing like that doesn't just dry up and take off with the breeze.' A large hand rose to stop the words forming on Tavener's mouth. 'Josh Allenby found him, then fetched Doc Brophy. You figure the rest.'

'All right,' Tavener broke in, suddenly tiring of the reprimand, 'so we made a mistake.'

McQuade's square face darkened. 'Another mistake was taking a little too much into your own hands. I still run things, let's not forget that.'

'Never been any question about it,' Tavener said quietly, stifling an anger that urged him to say what was really on his mind. 'Just that I thought you wanted him gone, and that was . . . .'

'But not that way.' McQuade's tone hardened. 'He had his chance to clear out and he didn't take it. Now I want to see him broken. I want him to watch me moving on to Shamrock, without being able to lift a finger to stop me.' As if having forgotten it was there, he regarded the cigar which had died between his thick fingers. 'After that, we'll see how good he is in a real fight, maybe facing someone like Royal.'

'Also thought,' Tavener said, looking straight across the desk at his employer, 'you were anxious to know who it was with the rifle that aided him.'

The busy grey brows pulled tightly together. 'So?'

Tavener hesitated. 'Claimed he didn't know. Said whoever it was took off soon's we was gone.' He rubbed thoughtfully at his jaw. 'Got a feeling he was telling it straight.'

'And might be,' impatiently McQuade ditched the cigar, 'he was lying through his teeth.'

'Not in the condition he was.' Shifting his position, Tavener leaned forward to stress his point. 'Like

I told you, he was near to being out cold when I got to him. He was in no condition to think straight, 'specially to make up lies.'

'Which doesn't change the fact that someone was up there, watching us threatening to string him up.'

Tavener shrugged. 'Probably some jasper who'd been waiting to hit the stage himself.'

'Maybe. But Prentice's about made up his mind it was us who stopped it. He's as much as said so.'

'O'Grady tell him?'

'Someone did. And my money's on him.'

Tavener's shoulders moved again. 'One man's word: he can't prove nothing.'

McQuade rolled back his chair. 'What about Alda and the other two?'

'Gone, but handy should we need them again.'

'We won't. Tell them to keep riding.' The office seemed to shrink when McQuade stretched up onto his legs. 'How bad was that beating?'

Tavener tried to smile. 'Be quite a while 'fore he thinks about climbing into a saddle.'

The sky was already dark, with a promise of rain, when O'Grady came into the house and flopped down on to the wide sofa in front of the fireplace. More than two weeks had passed since he'd been stoved up, and his body still wore bruises turned almost black. But the stiffness was gone and he was once again moving without having pain stab at him. Also fading were the marks on his face.

He fashioned a smoke, lit it, and inspected the room. It had been slow going, getting the house cleaned and back into the shape he was used to. Josh had made fairly regular visits, so had Walt Denton, who'd threatened to send out men to assist with some of the outside repairs. But, while it was comforting to know such help was on offer, he'd declined. And though he'd merely shaken his head, O'Grady knew that Denton understood his reasons for wanting to rebuild Shamrock wih his own two hands – though not his refusal to let him turn his crew loose to run down Alda and his cohorts.

Dan Prentice had been another visitor, one with questions. O'Grady told him only what he'd seen, nothing of what he'd heard, nothing regarding Mel Tavener and Red Scheil, and he wasn't sure why he did so. Unless the wall that had gone up between them was even higher than he'd realized.

By the second week he was riding again trying to determine how much stock he still had left. He was going to need at least one rider, that was obvious. Also money.

For now, though, he was in no rush. Whatever he did was done with care, while each day he waited for something to happen. And it would, he knew that with certainty. Those who had tried to ruin him would not quit simply because he'd returned.

Which was why, unlike in the past, there was always the Colt holstered against his thigh.

9

Joe Lennon pulled his gaze from the door of the private office and went back to the pretence of working. Something was bugging Washburn; that had been evident from the moment he'd arrived to open the bank, and it bothered Lennon not one bit.

On the other side of the closed door the banker slumped low in his chair, fingers nervously beating a tattoo on the desk top, mentally flogging himself for ever having become so involved with Ham McQuade.

Abruptly the finger-tapping hand closed into a fist that banged hard against wood. If he'd had any sense he'd have paid greater attention to the quietly voiced rumours concerning the man who'd taken over the old Ladder spread, a rugged stretch of tableland which its owner had long talked of selling.

When McQuade bought it for an undisclosed sum, people had laughed and called him crazy when he trailed his own herd up from New Mexico. Ladder range they said, would never hope to support that many cows. But there was no laughter when McQuade began buying up smaller sections of patented land, expanding his holdings until they reached down into the north-west of the basin, up against Maddy Denton's Box D, and O'Grady's Shamrock.

Long ropes and running irons, some opined, had provided both the herd and the capital brought to Tailgate. But it was said softly, for none could prove so. Just as there'd never been any proof that McQuade was behind the troubles suffered by those smaller ranchers who'd ultimately sold out to him.

Washburn whipped off his spectacles, rubbed away the smarting in his eyes. *How in the name of Hades had he permitted himself to fall so easily under the man's influence?*

The door to the office swung open, jerking him up straight, all set to bawl out Lennon for failing to first knock. Closing the door behind him, however, was not the teller, but the subject of his present anxiety.

'He been back to see you?' McQuade asked gruffly, dispensing with any form of greeting.

Washburn shook his head. 'No.'

McQuade dropped his huge frame into one of the clients' chairs. 'Well, he's back, already getting his place put together again, and for me that's not good news.' His eyes hardened upon the banker. 'If you'd had the guts to do as I told you, we'd—'

'Have bigger problems than we have now,' Washburn interjected. 'That idea was crude and dangerous, just like the one you pulled with the stage.' Seeing the cattleman's brows suddenly dip, his face darken, Washburn dredged up a sickly smile. 'I – I heard he ran into some trouble.'

'Heard something like that, too.' McQuade dug out a cigar and let the banker wait until he had it burning to his satisfaction. 'Seems like them three you hired to take care of his place jumped him when they got fired. Knocked the living hell outa him.'

Washburn's features took on a greyish hue.

McQuade blew smoke at the desk, watched it run

along the polished surface. 'Anyways, they're gone, and for your sake let's hope it's a long way.'

'*My sake?* Ham, it was you who told me to hire them!'

'Me?' McQuade stroked his moustache thoughtfully, eyes still like tempered steel. 'Now where in hell, boy, did you dig up a crazy notion like that?'

With that question Terry Washburn was given the answer to those he'd been asking himself. Fear had made him McQuade's ally, allowing himself to be so easily manipulated. Echoing inside his skull he could hear again the words which had first frightened, then swayed him to McQuade's side . . .

'It's like this, boy. I'll own the entire basin, make no mistake about that. When I do, either I'll be your most valuable customer, or I'll put you under.' Then his leather-like face had broken into a smile. 'Course, there'd never be need of it, not so long's you and me can see eye to eye on a couple of things.'

'You, you're dumping this all on me?' Washburn could feel a sticky dampness seeping into his shirt. 'My God, Ham. What am I supposed to do when he broaches me? And he'll do it. I know he will!'

'You'll think of something.'

A flash of anger swept through Washburn as he brushed at the cloud of smoke sailing into his face. 'And if he were to discover that they were hired simply to weed out the new crop of calves, transfer them to Slash, and . . . .'

'Hold it right there, boy!' McQuade's voice was like a mild clap of thunder. 'Sounds almost like you're accusing me of having had a hand in something not quite legal. All we did was take a down payment on what that son of a bitch owes me.'

Washburn struggled for words he couldn't find.

McQuade let him stew, finally propping heavy elbows on the desk. 'His cash position still the same?'

His answer was a curt jerk of Washburn's head.

McQuade's gaze tilted toward the ceiling, stayed there briefly. 'Good. Now I'll tell you what we're going to do.'

'Ham, listen . . . .'

'Yeah?'

'We've, we've gone as far as I want to go. Let – let's drop it.'

McQuade gave a sneering laugh. 'Sonny boy, when something's to be dropped, I'll be he one who tells you.' The lines in his face pulled stiff and straight. 'Now you listen, and you listen good.'

Washburn listened, hating every word that came at him, for each wrapped him still tighter into McQuade's scheme. Yet, somehow, when the other's voice stilled, there was courage enough to ask: 'Why, Ham? All because of what happened to Lance? Is that what it's really all about?'

For a while McQuade was silent, but when he hauled himself slowly out of the chair fires raged in his eyes. 'He killed my boy,' he said, face darkening, 'and by God he's going to pay for it, in a way that'll hurt more than any hangman's rope.'

He'd stripped the bunkhouse of everything left behind by Alda and the pair who rode with him, washed the grime from the windows, and mopped the floor. Grateful to have that sort of work behind him, he poured coal oil over the bundle of smelly clothes, tattered newspapers and magazines, and struck a match.

He was staring into the dying flames, thinking of Tim Becker, wondering what had happened to force him and the old crew to quit, when, drifting down from the wagon road came the clip of hooves and the light crunching of wheels.

The fire was reduced to a small black lump when the buggy entered the yard, headed for the house. He rolled down his shirt sleeves and went to meet it. But within the space of a single step his welcoming smile had already bit dust: the girl who sat waiting for him was not Susan Blayne, but the last person in the world from whom he would have expected a visit.

There were times, O'Grady recalled, when he'd have hurried to take her in his arms, but what he experienced now was the feeling of encountering a complete stranger.

When he reached the side of the buggy, her face devoid of expression, she said, 'Hello, Con.'

'Hello, Stacey.' He offered his hand to help her to the ground, but she shook her head.

'No, I won't be staying long.' Yet even as she said the words she was tugging at her gloves.

He let his hand fall. In every way Stacey Prentice remained a strikingly attractive woman, perhaps even more so than he remembered. She was wearing her dark hair differently now, gathered in an elaborate knot at the nape of her neck, and the hat, the dress and short cape were more stylish than anything he'd ever seen her in. The diamond ring was also a recent addition.

She studied him with a cool, almost regal-like aloofness, tiny glints starting up in the deep green of her eyes. 'Why did you come back, Con?'

The question seemed to carry a reprimand. He frowned up at her. 'Why not? This is my home.'

Lightly rouged lips thinned. 'Under the circumstances, I'd have thought you'd choose to make another start . . . somewhere else.' Before he could respond, she said, 'You've heard that I'm to be married?'

'Uh-huh. Congratulations. To Arnie as well.'

Her head moved in an offhand acknowledgment. 'I'm sorry it didn't work out for us.'

O'Grady shrugged. 'It's what you wanted.'

Quick anger put a flush in her cheeks. 'It wasn't, and you know it! It – it was you who – who went and ruined everything for us.'

He stared at her. 'What's it you came for, Stacey? An apology?'

Long-fingered hands fidgeted in her lap. 'I wanted to talk to you. About Arnie.'

He waited.

'Are you – are you going to hold it against him, the fact that he was obliged to testify at the trial?'

'There any need to?'

Her chin came up. 'None at all!'

'Then that's water gone down the hill.'

'Good. After all, Arnie did only what he had to do.' Her eyes sought his, searching for something that wasn't there. 'It . . . won't bother you . . . that you and I were—'

'Will it bother you?'

Colour spread from her cheeks, flooding her face. 'Of course not!' Clumsily she groped for the reins. 'Why should it?'

Not until she was more than a mile down the wagon road did Stacey Prentice finally relax her grip on the leathers. It had been a mistake going to see O'Grady; it would have been better to simply have ignored his return. Seeing her again had appeared to mean nothing at all to him, as if everything they'd once shared was no longer of any consequence.

She remembered when he'd been jailed, when Uncle Dan had asked if she were going to visit him, and the way she'd responded.

'No! Not after the way he's humiliated me in front of the entire town!' She'd flung herself onto the bed, sobbing. 'I hate him! I don't care what happens to him! *I don't! I don't!*'

And then she was thinking of Arnie, the man who would be her husband within a month. Quiet and caring Arnie; a pillar of the community, not a killer, not a man who'd earned himself time in prison. Arnie was everything Conner O'Grady could never be!

Again her hands tightened fiercely on the reins. 'Damn you, Con!' she cried loudly, tears pouring into her eyes. '*Damn you!*'

Each night, it seemed, Thadius Vinter was closing his store a little later than the night before. Not because he had business to keep him there, but simply because, at the end of the day, he was finding it more and more difficult to go home.

No longer was there any cheery greeting when he opened the front door, no longer did those warm, tantalizing odours trail Emily from the kitchen when she came to peck at his cheek. Now there was only silence, a cold and terrible silence.

It had been eight months since his wife died and, in spite of what well-wishers had promised, time still failed to ease Tad Vinter's tremendous sense of loss.

Standing in the doorway of his furniture store, he gazed out on to the darkened street, wondering if it might be best to dispose of the house, perhaps even the business, to go away, to . . . .

A despairing sigh shuddered through his body. *Go*

where? And to what? He sighed again, and set about locking up.

At the cafe he stopped for something to eat and exchanged brief words with Hannah Pettigrew, the proprietress, before starting for home.

Home for Tad Vinter – or the house which had once been home – was on the rise east of town, the section where Tailgate's more affuent citizens resided, where the houses were of a size, and spaced comfortably apart from each other.

The soft, slow clopping of a horse's hoofs reached him only when he was already halfway up the rise. He paused to glance over his shoulder, but there was no moon that night, barely a star in the sky, and he saw nothing. He resumed walking.

Whoever the rider was, he was much closer now, but still in no apparent hurry to get where he was going. Vinter kept walking, unreasonably nervous when the sounds he'd been listening to were almost upon him. Again he stopped, but before he could turn something smashed into his back, flinging him face-down into the dirt.

10

Slouched behind his scarred flat-top desk, Dan
Prentice finished packing his pipe, put away the
oilskin pouch, and hoped no one else would be
coming at him with questions he couldn't answer.
Ever since being called out the night before, and for
most of the morning, he'd been asking questions of
his own, and getting nowhere.

A resident living close to where Vinter had been
killed reported hearing a shot, going to the window
and seeing the vague shape of a rider disappearing
into the night. And that was it.

It made no sense, Vinter hadn't been robbed, and
he'd not been a man known to have enemies.

Tired and confused, Prentice struck a match, and
it was as if its flame threw light upon something he
should have remembered.

The afternoon was all but gone when, three days
later, Josh Allenby tied up at the corral near to where
O'Grady had been working. Inside the enclosure
four horses watched warily, as if questioning his right
to be there.

'Looking more like it used to be,' he grinned.

'Taking time,' O'Grady said, wiping his hands on a

kerosene-soaked rag, 'but slowly coming back together.' He jerked a thumb at the buckboard, the wheels of which he'd been greasing. 'Only now I'm out of supplies, so tomorrow it's a ride to town.'

Josh walked with him to the trough near the bunkhouse door. 'Stopped by a couple of times, but the place was deserted.'

O'Grady soaped his hands. 'Been riding. Trying to get an idea of what's still left.'

'And?'

'Darned few calves, and what remains of the herd is scattered to hell and beyond. Going to have to hire help to round them up, move them on to winter range.'

Josh glanced upward. Signs of the changing season were already there to be read in the sky. 'Nice job those jaspers did on you,' he muttered.

"Nice job they did for somebody.'

Josh made another slow inspection of the ranch yard, then brought his gaze back to O'Grady who was reaching for a towel hanging to the side of the trough.

'Seen Arnie yet?'

'No. Mostly just you and Walt Denton.' There seemed little point in mentioning Stacey's visit.

'He tell you what happened to old Tad Vinter?'

So far it had been a quiet morning. Too quiet, thought Joe Lennon; the kind of quiet that often precedes a storm. His eyes lifted to one of the broad half-curtained windows, thoughts returning once more to Thadius Vinter and the way he'd been gunned down. That was four days ago, and the sheriff, like everyone else, remained completely baffled.

Only just begun, his rumination was interrupted

by the closing of the street door, as Con O'Grady entered the bank.

'I'd like you to close out that account.' O'Grady shoved a small blue-covered book under the counter's brass grille. He heeled toward the railed partition, and before Lennon could speak was already barging into Washburn's office.

'Who turned off my credit, Terry?'

Blood draining from his pudgy face, Washburn struggled for a smile that died stillborn. 'What, what are you talking about?'

'Just come from Mossman's. He tells me my account's been closed.'

'Well . . . that's his prerogative, isn't it?'

'I hope so, Terry.' Frost in O'Grady's quiet tone put a brittle edge on his words. 'I'd hate to think someone'd pressured him into it.'

Washburn tried to laugh with as much success as he'd had with the smile. 'That's utterly absurd! Who'd do such a thing? And for what reason?'

'You tell me. Seems like Shamrock's credit was in good standing until I returned.'

The banker made a quick open-hand gesture. 'I'm sorry, but I'm in no position to explain the decisions any merchant might choose to make.'

O'Grady nodded. 'Maybe not.' Then slowly an eyebrow arched. 'Guess you've been told about the reception that was waiting for me when I got back to the ranch.'

For the first time Washburn seemed to notice the gun riding O'Grady's right hip. His head bobbed stiffly. 'I heard, and I still find it difficult to understand. There's never been trouble with any of those men before. *Never!*'

'Strange,' O'Grady frowned. 'Heard they cut up

rough with some of the Denton's hands. Tried the same with me the first morning I was back – even before they knew who I was.'

Washburn's tongue flicked at his lips, but before he could say anything O'Grady's voice was coming at him again.

'Thing I wanted your opinion on, is this. How come Alda and the other two were taking orders from Mel Tavener?'

'Tavener? No, that's not possible . . . .'

'He was there, Terry. Also Red Scheil.' The frost in O'Grady's voice turned suddenly to solid ice. 'Thing that's been bothering me is this. How come a crew you're supposed to have hired is taking orders from McQuade's lackey?'

'No . . . You're surely mistaken.'

'No, no mistake. Tavener was bossing the show.' A thin smile curved O'Grady's mouth. 'You and McQuade set it up, right? Installed those three so they could wreck Shamrock from the inside.'

'No, that's not true.'

'And now this business of freezing my credit . . . It something else the two of you cooked up?'

'Damn you! You can't come in here and – and make those sort of accusations!'

'Seems I just have.'

Shoulders slumping, Washburn released his breath and leaned across the desk. Above twisting lips the pale moustache resembled a mangled caterpillar.

'No amount of credit is going to help you now! You'll never get that spread back on its feet! So use your head and sell! Quit wasting your time: take what you can get and get out!'

O'Grady laughed softly. 'And that's what it's all about, isn't it?'

Still struggling for a reply, Terry Washburn realized he was once more alone. Swearing softly, he got up and slammed the door to his private sanctum, recalling only then that it had been wide open all the while O'Grady had been there.

Again O'Grady took the list from his shirt pocket, this time to place it on top of the bills he'd put on the counter. 'Shouldn't be any problem about filling that order now, should there?'

A tall man with narrow shoulders, wide hips and a balding, bullet-shaped head, Henry Mossman made no move to touch either list or money.

O'Grady glanced briefly around the store. It had always been large, but this morning it had the feel of something barn-like. 'What's become of Amy Brewster?'

'Left for Chicago, or some such place,' Mossman mumbled, reaching forward to push the small pile of bills away from him. 'I – I'm sorry. I can't.'

'Somebody leaning on you, Henry?'

No answer.

'McQuade?'

Mossman lowered his eyes.

'Henry, if I'm putting you on the spot, I'm sorry. If it helps any, tell him I held a gun to your head.' O'Grady sighed softly. 'Now get moving, will you? I need that stuff, but suddenly I can't wait to shake the dust of this town.'

Fifteen minutes later, satisfied that nothing packed on the buckboard would slide about and get damaged, he was closing the tailgate when he glimpsed a blonde head above a blue dress, moving briskly along the opposite sidewalk.

Just as he'd decided to leave the wagon where it

was and cross the street, he turned and came up hard against Dan Prentice.

'How long have you been standing there?'

'Long enough to see what's got your attention.'

'Then you'll excuse me.'

'She'll still be around after I'm through.' Prentice cocked his head a little to the left. 'Reckon you know about the shooting we had here in town.'

'Heard about it.' O'Grady nodded impatiently, meeting the older man's penetrating stare. When Josh Allenby had mentioned the shooting he'd had other things on his mind and hadn't paid much attention. Now he grew a little wary, wondering why Prentice had obviously gone out of his way to talk to him about it.

'Strange one,' the sheriff went on. 'Seems to be no reason for it. Nothing was stolen.'

O'Grady shifted his gaze, but nowhere on either side of the street could he now see the girl. He returned his attention to Prentice, shrugging.

'Sorry, Dan, I can't help you. I never really knew the man. Never had any dealings with him.'

'Think again,' Prentice said carefully. 'Your memory can't be that short. Tad Vinter was one of the men on the jury that sent you to prison.'

11

For a long moment O'Grady studied Prentice in silence. 'Anything more you got to tell me, Dan?'

A faint colouring flowed up into the sheriff's thin face. 'Guess not. Figured it was something you should know, is all.'

O'Grady gave a curt nod, said, 'Thanks,' and turned away to climb up on to the wagon seat.

If it had been Susan Blayne he'd glimpsed on the sidewalk, she'd now vanished. Silently cursing Prentice's intervention, he freed the reins and got the two-horse team moving in the direction of what he considered would be the girl's most probable destination.

But the school grounds were deserted, the building, with its doors and windows shut tight, offering no sign of occupancy. Which was just as well, for by then he'd had time to get a couple of things back into perspective. He had a ranch to rebuild, and, though yet with no real idea how he would do it, Gil's killer had still to be exposed. That, and a few other things that needed squaring.

Until then, however appealing he might find Susan Blayne, there was too much that still had to be done before his thoughts could be allowed the luxury of gravitating towards such a direction.

On a rise north of Main Street, a girl came out of the house and up to the porch railing, enjoying the wide, unobstructed view. Her eyes narrowed as she saw a wagon moving away from the schoolhouse.

The realization that it was Con O'Grady she was watching put shallow ridges into Stacey Prentice's brow. What business could he possibly have there? And why had he done anything but sit aboard the wagon, looking at the building?

A good while later she was still staring at the now empty road, trying to understand the reason for O'Grady's detour, when a flash of blue brought her gaze quickly around.

Susan Blayne, a small stack of books cradled in her left arm, walked purposefully up to the school's front door, unlocked it, and let herself in. Lips drawing tight, beginning to have a vague understanding of what she'd just witnessed, Stacey Prentice muttered a word she'd never dare to use in public.

A week after O'Grady had collected his supplies from Mossman, McQuade was still seething, threatening to put the storekeeper out of business if it was the very last thing he lived to do. But with the passing of another day, right after going through the few items of mail Red Scheil brought back from town, he became unusually withdrawn, snappish when spoken to.

On the desk, directly in front of him, lay a single sheet of paper he'd read several times since removing it from its envelope. Though by now he could almost recite the contents from memory, he picked up the letter and read it again, but on this occasion with all his thoughts centred hard upon the man most responsible for his recent ill-temper.

*

Leisurely building a cigarette, O'Grady sat on the veranda of his home, watching fast-falling shadows obliterate the signs of change that had been wrought since his return.

Behind his belt a simple meal sat comfortably, while every muscle in his body throbbed with what felt like the gentle beat of contentment, knowing the day's labour had achieved something. Like he'd told Josh Allenby, things were slowly coming together. From early dawn he'd been in the saddle, searching out strays, winding up with a gather which, though small, was better than expected.

It was going to take money to build the herd back into any semblance of what it had once been, but for the moment he was not overly concerned. He'd manage. Somehow.

He struck a match, touched the flame to the cigarette, drew smoke deep down into his lungs, and wished Gil were there this evening so he could talk of the work done, the many things still to be achieved. He wondered if in some way his brother knew just how much he was missed.

The cigarette smoked down to his fingers, he snuffed it out, flipped the butt over the rail, rose from the chair and went down the three veranda steps. He crossed the yard, walking with no destination in mind, images of Gil slumped in the buckboard floating before him. He also pictured Lance McQuade stretched out on the floor of the Ten Spot, his face hidden under the cloth someone had draped over it.

Mel Tavener had no idea why he should feel uncomfortable about having the Chinaman who cooked and kept house for McQuade summon him to the boss man's office. But tonight he did, and it irked him. He knew what had triggered off the old man's foul mood, just as he knew that what really had the inner fires raging was not so much the discovery that Mossman had provided O'Grady with everything asked for, but the fact that the storekeeper had disobeyed the direct orders of Hammond McQuade.

'Hoo Song says you wanted me,' he said, somewhat surprised at the sight of a bottle and glass on the desk. In all the years he'd worked for McQuade he'd never known him to be much of a drinker.

McQuade removed the cigar from between his lips, using it to motion toward a chair.

Tavener sat down, noting that the level of the whiskey had not been lowered to any marked degree.

'Been doing some deep thinking, Mel, asking myself a bunch of questions.'

Tavener's uneasiness began to grow.

'Like, for instance, what am I doing all this for?' McQuade's voice remained oddly soft when he looked up, directly at him. 'Lance's gone, and I got no other family. So why the hell am I doing it? Comes time for me to die, which's something we all got to do, what happens to Slash? Who do I leave it to?'

He waited, as if expecting Tavener to make a suggestion, going on when the foreman continued to remain mute. 'So what's the point in still trying to grow bigger? Why don't I just pack it all in, sell out and enjoy the years I still got left?'

Tavener sat up erect, not liking any of what he'd so far heard. 'Even knowing the one who killed your boy is still alive?'

'Been thinking about that, too . . . 'specially since this arrived.' McQuade pulled on the cigar, then picked up the letter responsible for his mood. 'Remember Gus Robey? He was tending bar at Carl Pickard's Ten Spot the night Lance died.' He flipped the single sheet of paper toward Tavener. 'Read it.'

Mention of Robey's name brought a sinking feeling to Tavener's gut. But it lasted only momentarily, replaced by an anger that fast dissolved into something that was a mixture of relief and satisfaction. For two years he'd been working up to this moment, not sure how to go about it afraid the wrong move would ruin everything. And now, without realizing it, the old fool slouched behind the desk had provided the opening he'd sought.

'Read it,' McQuade repeated, and when Tavener picked up the letter: 'Seems Robey's hit lean times. He's asking for money. A chunk of it . . . to keep his mouth shut about what really happened in the saloon that night.' His voice dropped to a feathery croak, he laid a granite-hard glare upon Tavener. 'You were there, Mel. So what's he saying? That things weren't exactly the way you and those other two told it?'

Without haste Tavener refolded the letter and tossed it casually back to his employer. 'Robey's no problem. He can't shoot off his mouth without risking charges of perjury, or worse.'

'That isn't what I asked!' McQuade's voice rose, became like a roll of distant thunder.

As if bored by the discussion, Tavener placed a hand across his mouth to stifle a yawn. 'OK, Ham, reckon it's time you got given the truth. Yeah, Lance was packing; everything happened just like O'Grady claimed in court. Why the hell did you think Robey was in such a hurry to leave town right after testifying?'

McQuade's leathery face became slightly bleached, the nostrils of his ample nose flared wide. 'Then you did strip Lance of his gun. You set up a frame for O'Grady, forced Robey to lie . . . .'

Tavener laughed scornfully. 'Don't act so damned shocked. You probably figured it from the start. You knew Lance went nowhere without that dandified gunrig.' Slowly he lifted his stocky frame out of the chair, hands digging deep into hip pockets while he smiled at the paled owner of Slash M.

'Few minutes ago you was asking who there was you could leave Slash to. Well you're looking at him. In fact, Ham, the time's arrived when you and me ought to talk real serious about a partnership. There's nobody deserves it more than me who's done most of your dirty work, who was always covering for your snot-nosed kid, dragging him out of one mess after another, because he was too damn stupid to . . . .'

The rest was never finished for in a single move Ham McQuade was rid of the cigar, out of his chair, and coming around the desk. Tavener was still pulling his hands free when McQuade's fist connected with the side of his jaw. He spun, trying to grab anything that would break his fall. His shoulder struck the wall behind him and gave his body another quarter turn before he went to the floor.

'Don't you ever again talk that way about my boy!' The words were a rasping hiss scraping through clenched teeth. 'You hear me? *Not ever!*'

Tavener pulled up on to his rear, confusion and anger in the eyes that glared upward.

'Yeah? Well, now. Ham, let me tell you about your darlin' boy! Let me tell you about the back-shooting bastard, and how he did for O'Grady's kid brother!'

*

Dinner over, Joe Lennon came out on to the narrow gallery of the boarding-house veranda to light one of the two cheap cigars he allowed himself each day.

A chill rode the night breeze, but he barely noticed it, his mind fully occupied with thoughts of the talk overheard when O'Grady had stalked into Terry Washburn's office, leaving the door wide open.

The exchange had confirmed much of what he already knew, things he had pieced together, and . . .

He was lifting the cigar back to his mouth when his hand froze. In the blackness of the alley facing the boarding-house, there'd been some kind of movement; something heard rather than seen.

Frowning, he took in a long drag of smoke, slowly released it, and, eyes straining in the dark, moved closer to the veranda rail.

12

The door of Hannah's Café was still closing behind Dan Prentice when the voice of someone stomping hurriedly toward him panted, 'Sheriff, over at the Ten Spot! Trouble's 'bout to break loose!'

Prentice sighed wearily. So far, with still a week to month-end and pay-day, that Saturday night had been reasonably quiet.

'What's it this time, Charley?'

'Allenby and that Scheil feller, they're getting set to tear each other apart!'

Not yet halfway there Prentice could hear the racket that told of a fight already in progress. Cursing not too softly, he quickened his pace.

Josh Allenby was on his hands and knees, picking himself up from the floor, when the sheriff brushed through the swing doors. Blood streaming from his nose and a cut above an eye, he appeared dazed, unaware that a grinning Red Scheil was closing in, measuring him for a kick to the chest or head.

Without breaking his stride Prentice drew and fired into the ceiling, bringing silence to the saloon. He levelled the Colt at Scheil. 'Step back!'

At the edge of the group crowded to the left of Allenby, two of his hands watched with angry and troubled expressions. On the other side, backs to the bar, stood at least three of the Slash crew.

Long face still twisted in a grin, Scheil shrugged, massaging the knuckles of his broad right hand. 'Still got a ways to go, Sheriff.'

'You heard me!'

'Aw, hell!' a voice complained loudly. 'Wasn't Red who started it! Let him finish it!'

'Shut up, Tavener!' Prentice snapped, gaze shuttling to Allenby, on his feet now, but wavering badly. 'What's it all about, Josh?'

Looking around the saloon, as if seeking out his opponent, Allenby seemed not to hear.

Prentice's gun picked out the pair of JA riders. 'Harry, you and Zack get him over to Doc.' He turned to where Red Scheil had shifted his bulk to the bar. 'And you, Scheil, get on home.'

Scheil's head hitched around, the rest of him unmoving. 'What for? It was him who . . . .'

'Don't make me repeat myself,' Prentice warned.

Mel Tavener bit short an objection when a smooth, very calm voice from the far end of the bar said, 'You heard the sheriff, Red. Unless you fancy spending the night in a cell, finish your drink and go.'

Scheil swore, but downed his drink, tossed the lawman a sneer, and strode for the door.

Tavener reached for his glass. 'Drink up, boys. Might's well ride along home with Red.'

Attired in a pearl grey suit and red brocade vest, a smiling Carl Pickard came up to Prentice. 'Put away the gun, Dan. It's over.'

'Why'd you allow it to get that far, Carl?'

Elegant shoulders rose and fell. 'Hell, it was hardly started when you arrived.'

'And exactly how did it start?'

The saloon owner set aside the smile. 'First let me buy you a drink. You look like you could use one.'

O'Grady extinguished the lamp, took down the Winchester racked near the front door, and went outside. He waited in the darkest corner of the veranda, listening to the dull thudding of hoofbeats drawing closer.

Only when the rider was part way into the yard, drawing rein as he hailed the house, did O'Grady step out of the shadows. 'Come on in, Walt.'

Denton rode up to the house, eyeing the carbine when he dismounted. 'Expecting visitors?'

'Never can tell. Especially this time of a Sunday evening.'

With the lights again glowing inside the house, Denton followed O'Grady into the kitchen, hooked out a chair from the table, and sat down, waiting while O'Grady shoved wood into the stove and got the fire blazing again.

'Starting to get back to the way it used to be,' he observed.

Moving the coffee-pot over the front plate, O'Grady asked, 'This is a sociable visit, Walt? Or's there something on your mind?'

Denton fingered his moustache. 'Anyone been around since last night?'

O'Grady shook his head.

'Then I guess you've not heard about Josh.'

A chill touched O'Grady's spine. 'What about him?'

'Last night, he got into a fight with Red Scheil, got himself pretty beat up.'

'Why?'

'I'll get to that,' Denton looked down at his hands rested on the table. 'Don't suppose you've heard what happened to Joe Lennon either.'

'Walt, you're the first person I've seen since last I was in town, and that's been a while.'

Denton nodded. 'The old feller was having himself a smoke when somebody perforated him with lead.'

Once more O'Grady remained silent, waiting.

'Way I got it from Prentice, he was outside his boarding-house when it happened. Those inside reckon they heard the shots, and the next thing they knew, Lennon's body was crashing through the front door.'

'And that's somehow got something to do with Josh getting beaten up?'

Denton shrugged. 'There was talk in the Ten Spot. Someone expressed a couple of opinions that rubbed Josh the wrong way. Told him to shut up, which's when Scheil stepped in. Wasn't what Josh had figured on, but seems like he wouldn't back down, even knowing Scheil could take him to pieces.'

'Hurt bad?'

'Haven't seen him. But from what Prentice tells me, it warranted sending him to Doc Brophy.'

'And these opinions Josh didn't care for?'

Denton swallowed more of the coffee. 'Concerned the way Vinter and Joe Lennon got themselves killed, the fact that both were on the jury that sat at your trial.'

The pot on the stove started making the right noises. O'Grady picked it up, filled two cups and slid one across the table. 'What's the rest, Walt?'

Before answering, Denton tasted the coffee and

nodded his approval. 'Trouble in the saloon started when one of the Slash crew suggested it was probably you who killed both Vinter and Lennon ... paying them back for the verdict they brought in.'

Denton released an irritated sigh when again O'Grady made no comment. 'Reason I rode over was to warn you there's even more talk going around now. Someone's stirring, spreading exactly what it was Josh tried to stem.' He raised his cup, emptied it, and let his gaze lock with O'Grady's. 'Got this uncomfortable feeling that Prentice could come a-calling before long.'

13

Except for a puffy lower lip, the cut above his left eye, and a badly swollen nose, Josh Allenby didn't appear to be in too bad a shape after his Saturday night brawl.

'Got suckered,' he grinned. 'Scheil moved in before I had my guard up. First blow dazed me, the second darn near scrambled my brain.'

O'Grady had ridden over early that Monday, arriving just as Josh and JA's three-man crew were leaving the cook-house. Josh coaxed him back inside and had the cook put together another breakfast.

Seated at the long, scrubbed table, O'Grady shook his head. 'You must've been either drunk or crazy to go up against him. 'Specially on my account.'

'Hadn't intended to,' Josh laughed softly. 'Was Herb Raiker I told to button up, and him I could've handled, easy. Scheil, though, made it sound like I'd insulted the whole darned Slash outfit, made it his fight.' Gingerly he fingered his nose. 'Reckon two weeks'll be time enough for this thing to shrink back to its regular size?'

The cook returned to dump a plate of bacon and fried potatoes in front of O'Grady and another with hot biscuits. 'Want more,' he grunted, 'holler.'

Alone again with Josh, O'Grady asked, 'Two weeks got some significance?'

Josh took a deep breath, expelling it in a soft, exasperated blast. 'Sorry. Should've figured you'd probably not be invited.'

O'Grady frowned, not understanding.

'Arnie and Stacey,' Josh explained. 'Just two weeks from now and they'll be tyin' the knot.'

Until learning that Josh and Arnold Allenby had been conceived by entirely different sets of parents, many had puzzled over the fact that in no way did the boys resemble each other. Whereas Josh was dark-haired and sturdily built, Arnie was fair and lacking somewhat in height, his round, boyish good looks spoiled by a fixed, brooding expression.

He'd heard about the shootings, the manner in which Tad Vinter and Joe Lennon had been gunned down, but he'd paid the news scant attention. Matters of greater importance had occupied his mind: foremost, his marriage to Stacey Prentice.

Then he'd been informed of the fight between his damn-fool half-brother and that lout Red Scheil, and it made him think again of Conner O'Grady.

Perhaps he should have gone to see him right after his return, explained that no personal animus had been involved, that he'd merely acted as a law abiding citizen, telling only what he'd witnessed the few minutes he was in the saloon, and not a word more.

Arnie pushed up out of the chair in which he'd been stretched, trying to read, but unable to do so because of a nagging feeling that, somewhere, something was not altogether right. He considered riding into town, to see Stacey, to make sure all was OK there . . . but again it was thoughts of the man at

Shamrock which thrust themselves to the fore.

It was nearly a week since Josh had been beaten up, but he'd done nothing about it, telling himself that if Josh's condition was in any way serious one of the JA crew would surely let him know.

The JA crew. An old anger flared swiftly. What had possessed his father to cut up the ranch and leave half of everything to someone who came from God-knows-where . . . a kid thought so little of he'd been dumped in an alley beside a saloon. All right, so Josh had been legally adopted, but that still didn't make him a true Allenby. And it never would, not in his sight.

The breeze which had sprung up earlier in the evening was starting to gain intensity, causing the curtains at the open windows to flutter irritatingly. Arnie started toward the window nearest to where he'd been seated, stopping abruptly as if encountering an invisible wall.

Across the sill, snout projecting into the room, a revolver barrel tilted upward. Arnie opened his mouth to scream a protest or plea that never cleared his throat. He heard the sharp report, saw the powder flash, and was already dying when the second shot struck home.

That same evening a noticeably changed Mel Tavener strode confidently into McQuade's office. 'Since when've you taken to riding at night?' he asked, one eyebrow hitched higher than the other. 'More important, where to?'

'Nowhere,' murmured McQuade. 'Just riding and thinking.'

'Meanwhile' – Tavener's voice dropped to a quiet snarl – 'I'm still waiting.' He waited some more and got back only silence. 'Well?' he snapped when, McQuade, chin slumped upon his chest, seemingly lost in his own thoughts, failed to lift his eyes.

Looking older by years, the lines in his face gouged deeper, the seated man emitted a quiet sigh.

'That story about Lance and Gil O'Grady. I've been wondering why I should believe it, Mel. All I've got is your word for what's supposed to've happened.'

'Not just mine,' Tavener said, head swinging from side to side. 'Raiker was with us. Ask him if I'm telling it straight.' Placing both hands on the desk-top, he leaned forward. 'The kid was sweet on that Amy Brewster; couldn't stand to think she preferred a nobody like O'Grady to him. Lance, he'd had a few before going around to her place that night, only what he'd not figured on was finding young O'Grady there. They had a fight, and he got the cream knocked out of him. When he came back to the Ten Spot he was a mess. Me an' Herb, we tried to get him to come on home, but he was having none of it. Started drinking again, worse than before.'

'You've already told me all that,' McQuade said stonily. 'I don't need to hear it again.'

'Yeah, well, perhaps you'd better, just so's you know exactly what kind of kid you raised.'

'Damn you, Tavener!' McQuade roared. 'If you think . . . .'

'I'm not finished,' his foreman cut in, a grin totally void of humour twisting his mouth. 'Listen again. Maybe it'll eventually penetrate.' From a box on the desk, he helped himself to a cigar and lit it. His grin widened as he looked down at the ashen countenance of the man who, for years, had paid his wages.

'OK, so finally we get the kid in the saddle, never

thinking we'll overtake O'Grady and that buckboard on the way home. Seems he must've also left town pretty late, and seeing him there turned Lance kind of crazy. He pulled ahead, yelling for O'Grady to stop, and instead got told to go to hell. Which's when he jerked iron, put two into O'Grady's back.'

Ignoring the copper receptacle, Tavener flicked cigar ash onto the floor, enjoying the sight of stifled anger in McQuade's narrowing eyes. 'So now you tell me, Ham, when do I see those papers?'

McQuade straightened a little, hands tightly gripping the arms of his chair. 'They're being drawn up. Should be ready tomorrow.'

'Better be,' Tavener flung back harshly. 'Already I waited too long for this. If I don't see something with my name and the word partnership on them, s'help me I take everything I know to Prentice.'

'Which would get you exactly what?'

Tavener came slowly around, for several seconds able only to stand with lips parted, at a loss for words. He knew, as did McQuade, that he couldn't go to the law, not without implicating himself. So far all he'd been trading on was McQuade's reluctance to have the truth of his son's death or his involvement in Gil O'Grady's murder, made public, preferring to keep everyone believing that Lance McQuade had been a good son, brutally killed in the prime of his life. He was still searching for a response when McQuade, managing a thin smile, said:

'See what I mean? You're in it just as deep, and you're still alive for the law to deal with.'

Inspecting the tip of the cigar, Tavener let his grin come slowly back to life. 'Could be, Ham.' He looked up. 'But where I go you go. Anyone should ask why I waited this long to open my mouth, I tell them I was working for you, that you threatened to . . . .'

The clatter of a rider arriving in a rush cut short the rest. Curious as to what it might mean, Tavener swung about and went out into the yard.

Minutes later he was back. 'Raiker just rode in with some interesting news,' he announced. 'Arnie Allenby's been shot dead, right inside his own home.'

McQuade's only reaction was a small twitching of heavy grey brows.

'Well now,' Tavener smiled. 'That could prove beneficial to us, right *partner*? What with all the speculation going on about O'Grady killing those other two . . . this ought really to put him out of our way.'

Laughing softly, the stocky foreman went back outside. Forehead deeply furrowed, McQuade reached slowly for his cigar while listening to footsteps crossing the yard and Tavener's voice loudly summoning Red Scheil.

14

Urgent knocking at the front door brought Stacey Prentice stiffly erect, the inexplicable sense of foreboding which had hounded her throughout the day suddenly a knot of apprehension in her chest.

With the aroma of freshly baked bread permeating the kitchen, she set aside the hot pan and the cloth used to protect her hands. She listened as someone struggled to keep his voice down while speaking agitatedly to her uncle.

Dan Prentice felt himself grow cold as he listened to the rider from Double A make his fumbling report. The man was still talking when, from somewhere at the sheriff's back, a soft, strangled whimper had him jerking swiftly around.

Halfway across the brightly lit sitting-room his niece stood with hands at her mouth, eyes wide and filled with horror. Prentice took a step toward her, but even as he moved Stacey's hands clenched into fists, and after that there was nothing he could do to quell the screaming.

Prentice felt as bad as the young man slouched on the other side of his desk looked. Not only had he been saddled with another killing, but this one had hit harder and much closer to home.

It had been a difficult night, with barely any sleep. Stacey's screams, the words squeezed out between racking sobs, still rang in his ears. It was the things she'd said that had him at the office now, waiting for Burt Udell, the temporary deputy, to bring the horses from Buchner's livery barn.

Making a production out of cleaning his pipe, he studied Josh Allenby, the last person he expected to find up and about while Tailgate was still in the process of throwing back the covers.

Josh had ridden to Double A immediately after being brought word of his stepbrother's death. But, after everything had been taken care of, instead of returning home he'd come back to town with the sheriff and Udell, aiming himself directly for the Ten Spot.

'Been trying to figure it out,' he mumbled, red-rimmed eyes upon the two carbines which had been taken from the rack and placed on the desk. 'Makes no kind of sense. What reason could there be?'

'If I knew the answer to that,' Prentice answered, thoughts centred elsewhere while feeding the pipe fresh tobacco, 'knew for certain, it'd make what I've got to do a whole lot more palatable.'

Josh squinted quizzically.

Prentice patted his pockets for matches. 'You know the talk that's going around; you even got into a brawl over it.'

'Come on, Dan, you don't believe any of that?'

'Trying hard not to. But last night, after hearing Arnie's been killed, Stacey went into hysterics, crying and carrying on no end. Claims she paid a visit on O'Grady, to tell him about her and Arnie. Says he got real mad; reckoned he still owed Arnie for his testimony, that he'd see him in hell before letting a wedding happen.' Prentice paused, at last locating matches in a desk drawer. 'Doc was there to hear it all. Had to send for him so's he could give her something to calm her down.'

For the length of a long breath, Josh was silent, then slowly his head moved in negation. 'No, Dan. Like you said, she was hysterical, probably not thinking straight.'

'Might be. But I got a duty to check it out.'

Eyes back on the two rifles, Josh scratched at a hollow, unshaven cheek. 'Looks more like you're going hunting.'

Pale and expressionless, Stacey sat propped up against pillows, watching and waiting while the blonde girl straightened her bed. Brophy had obviously been acting in her best interests when asking Susan Blayne to look in on her, but for reasons she was immediately hard put to explain, she wished he hadn't.

She'd seen her before, but this was the first time they'd met, the first time she'd been close enough to discover just how attractive Susan Blayne was. It was, however, an unappreciated discovery, as was the girl's friendly and easy-going manner.

She was remembering, too, Con O'Grady stopped outside the school, and how later she had seen this girl arrive. Again, for reasons which eluded her, she felt a surge of bitter resentment. She said, 'Doctor Brophy should not have put you to this trouble. It really wasn't necessary.'

Susan finished smoothing down the quilt. 'It's no trouble, none at all.'

No, she was not just attractive, but really quite beautiful. Hastily, Stacey shoved aside the thought. 'You've not been in town long, have you?'

'Just a few months.' And when Stacey's silence demanded amplification: 'I was teaching in Denver . . . until my parents died.'

'Oh, I'm sorry.' Then Stacey was frowning. 'But – but whatever on earth brought you to a place like this?'

Susan's response was a small smile, an equally tiny shrug. 'I was despondent; I thought a change—' She broke off with another quick shrug. 'There was a little money left to me, and when learning of a teaching post due to become vacant down here—'

Her curiosity satisfied, Stacey had no real desire to hear more. She gave a quick nod of understanding, at the same time allowing moisture to flood her eyes.

'Are you all right?' Susan asked, instantly concerned.

Lowering her head, Stacey let the tears roll. 'I – I suppose you know what happened?'

'As a matter of fact, I don't. Doctor Brophy simply asked me to . . . .'

Before she could finish a quiet sob broke from Stacey's throat. 'Last night my fiancé was murdered. Shot down in cold blood by – by that brute Conner O'Grady!' Unravelling a wispy lace handkerchief, she dabbed delicately at her eyes, oddly satisfied at the shock that washed across the girl's face.

And again it bothered her that, rather than grief, Arnie's death had left her with a combination of anger and frustration, a feeling of having been cheated. Twice she'd been on the threshold of marriage and twice her plans had come to naught.

'No!' Susan's rejection of the charge was almost

automatic. 'There's surely some mistake. I've met Mr O'Grady . . . .'

Stacey pulled herself up straight, pressing stiffly against the pillows. 'But I doubt you know him quite as well as I do. There was a time,' she went on, tone grown abruptly brittle, 'when I even believed we'd marry. But then he went and killed someone in a disgusting saloon brawl that earned him a term in prison. He – he blamed Arnie for helping to send him there.'

When first she'd voiced that lie there'd been the mild taste of remorse. Now there was nothing.

Susan remained unruffled. 'I've heard about that; also the conditions under which he was—'

'Are you doubting my word, calling me a liar?'

Like a flash of lightning, remembering what had really transpired when she'd driven the buggy out to the O'Grady ranch, came understanding of both her anger and the lie. This girl, staring at her with that stupid, stunned look spread across her face, might yet have the man on whom she'd so easily turned her back . . . while she . . . *she'd lost everything.*

'No,' Susan murmured, totally confused by the mercurial mood change she was witnessing, 'but—'

'But what? He killed the man I was to marry, and, and you have the gall to stand there and defend him?' Tears discarded, in a spurt of fury, Stacey threw back the covers and was out of the bed. 'I think you had better leave, right now!'

That morning, in his office at the Ten Spot, Carl Pickard was having trouble with the composition of a letter when the door opened to admit a stone-faced Ham McQuade. Carefully he put aside pen and paper, trying to rake up a smile.

McQuade shut the door, dropped his heavy frame into one of the vacant chairs and, taking three long pulls on the freshly lit cigar, laid his gaze hard upon the saloon-owner. 'We got some straight talking to do, Carl.'

Freezing the smile, Pickard shrugged. 'Thought that's the way we always did it.'

'Then tell me again what happened here the night my boy died. And this time I want the truth.'

Pickard took on a hurt expression. 'I don't get it. It's like I told Prentice and anyone else who wanted to know, I was here, in my office. Time I got there to see what was going on, it was all over.'

'Carl,' McQuade said tightly, 'I'm in no mood for a runaround. You talk to me, or you may never be the same man after I walk out of here!'

With an open-handed gesture of despair, the saloon owner leaned back. 'All right, Ham,' he sighed. 'But I don't think you're going to like it.'

Still later, after a long time spent with Tailgate's only lawyer, Hammond McQuade had only just stepped on to the sidewalk when he heard someone calling his name. Turning, he found the waddling figure of Terry Washburn coming at him.

'Have you seen this?' Round face flushed with exertion, Washburn unfolded the four-page newspaper he carried. 'Looks as if you may soon be getting what you want.' He thrust the paper into McQuade's hands. 'Take a look. Last night Arnold Allenby was killed, and suspicion's full upon O'Grady.'

Though he'd already had the news from the lawyer, McQuade took the paper and briefly scanned the headline. Slowly he refolded it, shoved it into a coat pocket, and walked away without having said a single word, leaving the rotund banker to stare after him in open-jawed consternation.

In a veil of steadily darkening grey, a weary Dan Prentice and the lanky Burt Udell stood in the large front room, hats in hands, awkward and uncomfortable in the presence of an angry Maddy Denton and her son.

'I'll tell you again,' she said scornfully, seated in a straight-backed chair, left hand tight around the stick held erect between her knees, 'had Con been around – which he hasn't – we'd've given him any help he needed. But if you believe he'd be so stupid as to do anything like that, right after getting let loose from prison, you've less sense than I ever gave you credit for. Especially,' she added bitterly, 'when he was sent there for something he never did.'

'Maddy—'

'He never killed young McQuade, not deliberate. Which, Dan Prentice, you darn well know!'

'What I know and what the court decided—'

'And what you're doing right now seems to be nothing but a repeat performance of everything that's gone before.'

'Ma's right,' Walt Denton said, standing protectively next to his mother's chair. 'Con's no killer, and for sure no sneaking bushwhacker. If he wanted to settle any score he'd do it out in the open, not skulking around in the dark.'

'Walt,' Prentice sighed. 'I can understand your and Miz Maddy's sentiments, but the fact remains, he's had the best reason of anyone we know. Stacey heard him make threats, and there's this.'

Walt started to speak but Prentice made as if he hadn't noticed. He took a breath, wishing he was anywhere but here confronting this stern-faced woman and her boy. 'Me and Burt we been searching for him all day, but with no luck. We were started back, headed here, when we crossed trails with one of McQuade's crew.' Prentice hesitated knowing that what was to follow would not be well-received. 'He had something of interest to relate.'

Both Dentons waited, offering no hint of what they might be thinking.

'Seems,' Prentice continued, 'last night he was sent with a message to Double A. Almost there he heard a couple of shots. Next thing there's someone aimed his way, travelling like a turpentined cat. Guessing something to be wrong, Scheil pulled into the brush, let whoever it was ride on past.'

'*Who'd you say?*' The question was a quiet explosion from Walt Denton.

Reluctantly, Prentice told him.

Denton's laugh was of quiet disgust. 'And you're ready to swallow something the likes of Red Scheil tells you?'

'He's prepared to swear to what he saw.'

'Which would make some difference; for two bits he'd swear he'd seen a polka-dot cow.' Walt's voice lowered. 'Let me take a shot at what he's supposed to have seen, Dan. It was Con, coming from Arnie's place, wasn't it? Probably with a smoking gun still in his hand!'

15

Concealed in the shade of clustered pine, O'Grady looked down the long slope at two figures moving cautiously from one building to the next. Prentice he recognized, but not the lanky one with him.

He'd have continued on down, to find out what they wanted, but for the fact that their manner and movements were not suggestive of a social call. Walt Denton had warned of the possibility of such a visit, and so he stayed put, waiting until both men finally returned to their saddles.

The direction of their departure, though, was not back toward town, but along a trail that would take them into the heart of Shamrock, eventually to the section he'd been working.

Plainly, Prentice and the man who was probably his temporary deputy, were looking for him. And geared for trouble. Which meant something more must have happened since Walt's warning, something of which he had no idea, but for which they apparently already had him notched and branded.

When locating the stone between hoof and shoe which had started the roan limping, he'd chastised himself for not having brought along a reserve mount. Now, appreciatively, he patted the neck of the animal beside which he stood. If he hadn't been forced to return and switch horses, Prentice and the deputy would probably have rode in on him while he'd been preoccupied with other problems.

Not until the lawmen were out of sight did he start down to the corrals, wasting no time once there in transferring his saddle to a blaze-faced sorrel.

Once before he'd submitted to the law, believing truth and justice would ultimately prevail. Instead, lying witnesses, and Hammond McQuade's ability to buy co-operation and apply pressure where it counted had cost him two years of precious freedom. It wasn't going to happen again: not if he had anything to do about it.

In the house he tossed food into a sack and jammed a change of clothes and a box of .44 cartridges into saddle-bags. In a manner he could not yet comprehend, events were shaping up against him, but even as they did there grew an odd awareness of somehow being drawn nearer to the end of something which had started a long time ago.

All of which was a stretch down the road yet, and the way there could prove pretty rocky.

Clear of the yard, he reined to a brief halt, unsure of his destination. It was only natural that his first thought would be of the Dentons. But with no desire to involve either Maddy or Walt in his problems, the notion was abandoned. He considered Old Town and was almost decided to head there, when suddenly he was smiling grimly.

Slack in the saddle, a weary Burt Udell mopped sweat from the back of his long neck and frowned at Dan Prentice. 'Ready to accept he's long gone?'

'Burt's right,' a rider stationed close to the deputy

growled. 'Weren't so, we'd've found evidence of it.'

Prentice was almost inclined to agree. For nearly two full days he, Udell, and three recruited men had scoured Shamrock and Box D terrain without turning up so much as a hint of their quarry. But, knowing O'Grady better than any of them, Prentice remained convinced he was still somewhere out there.

Udell lifted his eyes to a sky the sun had deserted. 'Can we call it a day?'

Prentice performed a slow surveyal of the men who by pre-arrangement were met up back in Shamrock's yard, reading the expectancy on the faces of each. Guess so. Not much else we can do today.'

'Ask me,' grumbled another, 'tomorrow'll be no different. Wherever he is, it ain't nowhere around these parts!'

Slash had been fast to offer their help in running down O'Grady; help which Prentice had no option but to accept. At the time too much else occupied his mind to think about it, but that the offer should come from Mel Tavener and not McQuade had struck a curiously sour note.

That they too had so far come up empty-handed did not sit well with Tavener. When the four assigned to the search rode in that evening, he was out in the yard to meet them.

Stopping ahead of the group, Royal Janner cuffed back his hat, sunken eyes harsh and resentful. 'Same's yesterday,' he spat down at Slash's new partner. 'Not a cussed thing!'

From the dark shadows of the gallery, Ham McQuade watched expressionlessly as Janner swung his horse away, knowing what disappointment and anger churned away inside of Tavener. Within days of having taken one successful and profitable step, Tavener's ambition was showing considerable growth. Already he was viewing the basin from the same angle as he, Hammond McQuade, had once done.

Stomping back to his quarters, the ex-ramrod, who was still thinking about moving his gear into the main house, braked, and stiff-legged it back to where the returned riders were unsaddling.

By the time the rest of the crew rolled in for breakfast, Herb Raiker had already been forty minutes grudgingly riding what had once been Ladder range, the first of McQuade's Slash holdings.

He was slope-shouldered, with the coarse black hair of an Indian; an inner rage pulled the skin tightly over his long, flat face. Silently he cursed Tavener for dumping this chore on him. It was something any of the others could have done, so why pick on him?

He'd never liked it up here; always it left him feeling naked, exposed to predatory eyes watching him from behind every rock and thicket. This morning, forced to ride with chin tucked in, eyes slitted to reduce the cold sting of the wind, he hated every stinking thing about the place.

Where the trail he followed swung right, dipping between giant boulders, he nervously paused again to check his back trail, ears straining to hear above the wind's woeful murmuring. Ever since reaching the mesa he'd been spooked by the feeling of having a shadow traipsing at his rear, occasionally reaching out to lay a cold finger along his spine.

Damn Tavener for insisting he make the ride alone! He could swear that at one point he'd heard the soft snort of a horse ... another time what sounded like a shod hoof nicking stone ....

Raiker started down the sandy, well-worn incline that broke through rock and heavy brush, twisting down to a narrow stream, so shallow the water seemed not to move. Traces of ice were already starting to show along its edges.

His slitted gaze lifted to the far side. A mile or so beyond the slow rise was the three-room cabin where the McQuades had once lived.

Not until his eyes were again scouring the ridge, did Raiker realize he'd stopped. He'd have sworn he'd seen movement up there ... a horseman paused for just a moment against the open grey sky. Still uncertain, but ready to pass it off as trick of wind and light, he got the animal under him back into motion.

Almost at the stream, he was again hauling back, when the sight of the rider suddenly stepping his horse out of the brush caused him to yelp.

He'd been right; someone *had* been trailing him. They had guessed his destination and rode on ahead to wait.

The rider in the deerskin jacket nodded toward the land at his back. 'On your way to fetch in help?'

Raiker barely heard the question. The gun pointing at his middle commanded his complete attention.

16

Numbed by fear and confusion, Raiker tried to make
sense of the impossible. If this was the man he'd spotted on the ridge, how had he been able to get down
here so fast, and without being seen?

'I know what's back there,' he heard O'Grady say.
'And who's using it.'

'Wasn't my idea,' he croaked, words barely reaching above the noise of the wind-rustled growth
surrounding them. 'Mel sent me to call 'em in. I'm
just following his orders.' He squinted hard at
O'Grady. 'How – how long you been trailing me?'

'Long enough.'

Inadequate shoulders slumped. 'No wonder they
couldn't find you. All the time you been right there
in their backyard!'

The guess was somewhat off-centre, but accurate
enough to let it ride. O'Grady himself could still not
fully understand why, when departing Shamrock to
avoid a confrontation with the law, he should
suddenly think of Slash territory as probably the last
place anyone would think of looking for him. It had
been years since last he'd travelled that far across the
range once held under the Ladder iron, back when
Ham McQuade was still an unknown quantity.

He tilted the .44. 'Don't make it sound like you were no part of it, Herb. I've done some riding myself; seen you loping along behind Janner.'

'I had to. You know Tavener. He gives an order—'

'Why?'

'Why . . . what?'

'What do they want with me?'

Raiker's brow slowly creased. 'Why'd you think? For killing Allenby. Him and those other two: Lennon and Vinter.'

In the wind tugging at his clothes, O'Grady discovered a sharper chill. 'Josh. . .?'

'I'll go to hell! You don't even know . . .'

'I asked a question,' O'Grady snapped, and the other's hands made a grab at higher air.

'Not him – the other one – the brother.'

The cold took a deeper bite. 'When was this?'

Raiker told him. 'Way they got it figured you been paying off in lead those who testified against you – had a double reason for killing Allenby, him set to get spliced to someone'd been your girl.'

'How do you figure it, Herb?'

'I don't! I got no opinions. I follow orders, is all.' Performing another squirming shift in the saddle, Raiker let his voice become a thin whine. 'Listen, maybe you and me we never exactly seen eye to eye, but I never once . . . .'

'Aren't you forgetting how your bunch tried to lynch me?'

'No!' A furiously wagging head backed the denial. 'McQuade was just fooling, he only wanted to scare you, keep you clear of Tailgate!'

'And the beating I took the day I returned to my spread? That another gag?'

'Not me! I was nowhere near! It was Mel and Red!

Them and Alda and . . . .' He broke off, seeing the smile break slow and cold across O'Grady's face. 'It's the truth; I swear it! I wasn't with 'em!'

'Then tell me about Tim Becker.'

The question caught Raiker off guard. He started to say something, then his eyes narrowed and his jaw clamped shut.

'I'm being hunted for murder, Herb. Assuming I'm guilty . . . reckon your life would make any difference to what happens to me?'

It was as if Raiker had found something alive in his gullet when he tried to swallow. Head again in a slow left to right swing, he said, 'I had no hand in that neither. All I know's what I heard Royal and Mel talking about when they thought no one else was around. Tavener reckoned that if Becker disappeared the rest of your crew would drift.'

He tried again to get rid of what was in his throat. 'I've told you everything, I swear! Rest is just things picked up. They'd done for Becker, that wasn't hard to figure; buried him under a rock slide, I think.' Slowly, Raiker's shoulders began to lift. 'That's it. You want more, go ask them.'

O'Grady had not been blind to the sudden change in attitude, nor the lids lowering over dull eyes, covertly flicking to perhaps the source of new found courage. With the touch of winter flooding through him, he gave in to instinct, booted the sorrel into a sharp right turn, flinging himself from the saddle at almost the exact moment a voice at his back barked:

'Drop the—!'

In the middle of the command a gun thundered twice. But by then he was on his feet, Colt drawn and searching. The third shot came so close it felt as if it had caressed his cheek in passing.

On the other side of the stream, close enough to have heard the exchange between himself and Herb Raiker, a thickset, instantly recognizable figure, sent off one more hasty shot before scrambling back to cover.

Twice O'Grady triggered the .44, achieving nothing. He fired again, a split second before the gunman would have been lost from view. The squat figure made a loud, grunting noise, and then it was as if a catch rope had found his neck and jerked him to the ground.

Without warning a third gun spoke up loudly, its owner taking greater care about aim. Hot metal sliced O'Grady's upper left arm, shock and impact spinning him off his feet.

In a scrambling crawl he succeeded in securing temporary protection, while still clinging to the .44. His gaze scoured the opposite ridge. Whoever was up there was keeping well out of handgun range.

Lead whanged off the rocks behind which he lay, letting him know it would be only a matter of time before one of the slugs found its target.

Ramming gun into holster, he rolled on to his side. Legs braced under him, suddenly conscious of the burning pain in his wounded arm, he rose in a low crouch, charging to where the sorrel stomped and danced nervously. Grabbing up dragging reins he hauled himself awkwardly into leather, for the first time aware of the wet warmth leaking out from under his shirt cuff, spider-webbing over his left hand.

He spotted the riderless mount almost up the sandy slope, and wasted a precious moment twisting around to look for Raiker. He found him staring wide-eyed at the grey morning sky. Dark stains which hadn't been there previously glistened across the front of his canvas jacket.

Were it not for Raiker's changed attitude signalling something wrong, the slugs which had killed him would almost certainly have gone where intended. Instead, in missing, they'd found another target seated squarely in their path.

The sharp-featured lightweight held his place long after O'Grady had vanished. His name was Hurd Drury, part of the trio the banker Washburn had hired to replace the Shamrock hands. He knew one of his shots had scored a hit, was sure O'Grady would not return, but still he waited, fearful of a possible trap.

He listened to the howls and curses of Fred Alda, somewhere in the brush below. Ignoring the cries for help, his gaze would now and then stray to where Herb Raiker had fallen. Each time it did his gut froze up.

Mutely he cursed Alda. Had he simply fired instead of wating time with words, they wouldn't be where they were now.

'Get down here, damnit!' Alda rasped painfully. 'I'm bleedin' like a stuck pig!'

Still the lightweight refused to stir.

Long minutes staggered by. Jowled face awash with sweat, Alda tried again to shout, and found his throat had gone dry and stiff. Then he was grabbing up the gun put down beside him, bending his neck toward what sounded like the scrape of boot leather.

'Get me out of here,' he croaked angrily, finding the bantam-size Drury stooped close by. 'I'm losin' too much blood. Need a doctor.'

Hurd Drury studied the neckerchief knotted

around Alda's fleshy thigh. Like the leg of the tightly
stretched jeans, it was drenched and not doing much
good.

He considered the problem of going back up the
slope for Alda's horse, of getting him loaded into the
saddle. He wished Ollie Bascombe, the third of their
group, hadn't got restless and cut out. It'd be easier
to decide things were Ollie on hand.

'That was a Slash man you killed, Fred.'

'It was an accident, dammit!'

'Think Tavener and the others will believe it?'

Alda groaned, squirming around so he could look
at Drury without having to keep his neck twisted.
'Dammit, you were here! You saw how it happened!'

'Think it'll help?' Drury moved his eyes back
across the shallow stream. 'Wonder what he wanted?'

'The hell with that!' Alda bellowed, finding new
vocal strength. 'Fetch my horse! Help me out of . . . .'
He broke off when Drury's head began a slow sway.

'Don't think so. Don't reckon I'm that keen to
have Tavener get the wrong ideas, like we was maybe
pulling a double-cross.' The rifle began to angle. 'It's
like you always told me, Fred; a man's gotta look out
for himself.'

A stifled curse rattled from Alda's parched throat.
Before Drury knew what was happening the gun in
Alda's fist was raised and pointed, flame smearing its
muzzle.

The lightweight was sent stumbling backwards,
finger tightening on the rifle's trigger.

17

Red Scheil lay with hands folded behind his head, deaf to the snores rumbling through the bunkhouse, trying to make sense of the day's events.

So they could lend a hand in the search for O'Grady, Raiker had been dispatched to fetch in the Alda bunch. By noon, when he'd still not returned, Tavener had sent Janner and him to find out why.

It was kind of a shock, coming across Raiker, asprawl like that, chest torn open. An even bigger one finding Alda and the dime-sized punk, dead on the other side of the stream. It wasn't hard to surmise what had happened there. Why it had, that was something else. And if it was one of them who'd shot Raiker, it made for yet another question.

His gaze slid through the dark, to the bunk in the far corner of the room. Janner'd been quieter than usual on the ride back. Was he also awake, maybe thinking the same kind of thoughts, puzzling over those other prints they'd found? Scheil wished he had a bottle. A few drinks might bring on sleep.

Another who'd experienced difficulty getting to sleep was Ham McQuade. But it was mostly anger that kept him awake. He'd told Tavener to get rid of Alda and his companions. Instead, believing they

111

might still be needed, he'd kept two of them stashed away. Now, in a way that made little sense, both were dead. Along with Herb Raiker.

Sleep, when finally it overtook him, produced disjointed dreams of happier, almost forgotten times. Then, like a candle snuffed out in a breeze, the dream was ended and he was sifting the night sounds, trying to discover what had woken him.

Against his temper came the gentle pressure of something very hard. 'Not a sound!'

The man in bed released trapped breath. Eyes flicked sideways, but he could see nothing. 'What do you want?'

'How about we start with you telling me where you had Tim Becker buried?'

McQuade went stiff under the blanket. 'What the hell makes you think I'd—?' He broke off sharply, disbelief instantly replacing the anger in his gravelly tone. 'O'Grady . . . that you?'

He got no answer, but the pressure of the gun was removed. 'You got the gall to sneak into my home and hold a gun on me!'

'Sorry. Guess I should've waited till daylight and made it easier for your bunch to jump me.'

McQuade shut up. His vision was adjusted, enabling him to make out the man who'd taken a step away from the bed, standing with the closed door at his back.

'Ran into Herb Raiker this morning,' O'Grady told him. 'He spilled what he knew. Now you tell me the rest.'

It wasn't much, the pale moonlight seeping through the open window, but enough to expose the frowning, hawk-nosed face of McQuade elbowing himself up against the headboard. 'You the one killed him?' he asked, remembering Janner's report of an extra set of hoofprints near to where they'd found Raiker's body, prints that told them nothing, led them nowhere.

'If you want to know how he died, ask those skunks holed up at your old place. He got what was meant for me.'

'Be hard to do,' McQuade returned, straining to find an expression on the other's face that might tell him something. 'They're also dead.'

O'Grady's brief silence was the only suggestion of possible surprise. 'Tough,' he sighed. 'But right now I'd sooner hear about Becker.'

McQuade cleared his throat irritably. 'All right! I'll not deny I gave orders to send him and your crew packing, but that's all.' He sat up still straighter. 'Like it or not, that's the truth. I've had to do some killing in my time, but no one's ever been able to call it murder.'

More than can be said of your son, O'Grady thought, left arm throbbing more fiercely than ever, making him impatient to finish what he'd come for, and be gone.

'Janner and Tavener took care of it,' he said. 'And they get their orders from you!'

Red Scheil pulled on his boots, and quietly let himself out of the bunkhouse. He rolled a cigarette, pondering again the delights of a glass at his lips, liquid fire trickling down to his gut, smoothing the edges of his nerves. He lit the cigarette, drew smoke deep into his lungs, ambling aimlessly across the yard.

Damn, but he could use a couple of stiff snorts!

The night was cool, with little moon. A breeze

stirred leaves, drew creaks and rattles from things he could not see, on which he wasted no thought. He paused, eyes upon the house, wondering why Tavener was taking so long to move in. If it were him there would be no dallying. Not when it meant a soft bed in a room of his own, a place where a man could put up his feet.

Scheil took a slow, final puff on the smoke before grinding it underfoot. He was still looking at the house, remembering something . . . .

Moments later, he was back in motion, this time moving with purpose to the rear of the building.

No locked doors hindered entry, nor did he have any difficulty, even in the dark, finding his way to the big front room where he knew McQuade kept his liquor.

Running a hand over satin-smooth doors, he felt for the latch, careful to make no noise in case he disturbed the old man.

Thought of such a thing brought a grin to his mule-like face. What the hell did it matter if he did wake up? Things had changed; Mel was part owner now and, with the whole crew behind him, these days it was mostly what he said that went.

He was quietly closing the cabinet door when a sudden noise paralyzed his hand. Believing nerves or imagination to be playing tricks on him, he stood dead still, ears sharply cocked.

Then, still holding on to the bottle, he started for the short passage which led to three bedrooms as stealthily as his bulk would allow. At McQuade's door he bent his head closer to the wood.

He'd been right! He hadn't been hearing things. Someone was in there, talking with McQuade . . . *and he didn't have to see any face to know who it was!*

Free hand dropping to his side, Scheil pulled up straight, remembering too late that his holstered gun hung from a peg in the bunkhouse. Silently he turned, plotting the location of McQuade's gun rack in his mind.

'I told you once,' McQuade said coldly, wiping a hand over his thick moustache, 'I had nothing to do with Becker's death, if he's dead, and I sure as hell had no hand in killing those three! What would I have to gain from it?'

'Maybe a whole lot. The first two who died were on the jury that convicted me, and Allenby was one of the key witnesses. Whoever killed them rightly figured I'd be the first person the law would think of, seeing it as some sort of cockeyed revenge.' O'Grady shifted his position slightly: the injured arm felt as if it were on fire. 'With me permanently out of the way this time, you could grab up Shamrock with a whole lot less effort, then concentrate on taking over the rest of the basin.'

'Get something straight,' McQuade snorted. 'If I'd wanted you dead, there's easier ways it could've been handled, and it'd have happened long ago.' But even as he spoke he was thinking of Mel Tavener. The kind of twisted scheme that had been spread out before him was just the sort a mind like Tavener's might cook up. 'Now, I'll tell you for the last time; I had nothing to do with any of those killings!'

'And if I had, your name would've topped the list. You're the one who's owed the most!'

'That why you're here, to get me?'

'Be kind of stupid, doing that, when I didn't kill any of the others. Guess I only wanted to hear something.'

'And?'

'Don't know. Don't know why I should, but this time I actually find myself believing you.'

'Then,' McQuade sighed quietly, 'you may as well hear this. The night Allenby was shot—'

There was no time to finish. O'Grady was suddenly stepping away, barely having reached the side of a tall bureau when the bedroom door slammed violently against the inner wall.

'Freeze! Anyone so much as takes a breath, he's dead!' The bulky figure framed in the doorway listened intently. 'Ham, who you got in here with you?'

'You damned idiot!' McQuade growled tightly. 'Just what in hell do you think you're up to?'

Scheil paused, flicking an uncertain glance at curtains stirring at the open window. 'All right,' he said, taking a cautious step into the room, something apparently decided. 'Get a light.'

The rest became a startled curse when, out of the corner of an eye, he caught a shifting of light, no more than a weak reflection in the bureau mirror of curtains again disturbed by a breeze.

In a single movement he whirled and fired.

18

Under the impact of the first bullet the mirror disintegrated. O'Grady thrust himself away from the wall, hearing McQuade's furious, protesting bellow get lost in the racket of Scheil's gun.

Pivoting at the middle, trying to locate the piece of darkness he'd seen break away from beside the bureau, Scheil's cursing turned into a thin, choked cry when the curtain suddenly billowed inward, allowing a pale shaft of light to reveal a figure placed only yards in front of him. Iron bucked wildly in his fist, but shock and fear threw his aim wide.

With the echo of his own shot rumbling in his ears there came a sledge-hammer blow to his hip, driving him through the doorway on legs he could no longer control.

To the accompaniment of Scheil's whimpering, O'Grady moved swiftly to the windows. Jerking aside the curtains he flung a look at the bed, swallowing the words almost upon his lips. McQuade was toppled on to his side, anaemic moonlight pouring through the uncovered window exposing the blood trickling down the side of his face.

For a moment he could only stare. He'd fired a single shot, but there was no way he'd be able to prove it was not his bullet that had struck McQuade.

Disregarding the yells coming from the bunk-house, he stepped back to the bed, in time to hear a tiny almost inaudible moan escape from the limp form.

Keenly aware of boots pounding the yard's compacted surface, O'Grady left McQuade as he was, returned to the window and swung a leg over the sill. It was not the way he'd entered, but right then it seemed a more suitable exit.

The short drop to the ground sent pain jarring down the length of his injured arm.

He'd left the sorrel far enough from the house so that any sound it might make would probably not be heard. It whickered now when he freed reins, pawing ground as he swung to saddle, seemingly as anxious as he to be moving. Men's voices, one of them screaming orders, drifted their way as they turned their backs on the Slash M buildings.

At the front door of the house Mel Tavener watched while Scheil, groaning and complaining, was carried on a makeshift litter and loaded on to the prepared bed of a spring wagon. Wordlessly, the ranch cook who'd helped with the carrying, climbed up on to the driver's seat. Hoo Song, for years McQuade's personal servant, frowned up at Tavener.

'Wha' 'bout boss? Wha' happen him?'

Tavener adopted what he hoped was a forlorn expression. 'Best to leave him like he is for the time being. Give the sheriff a better idea of what happened.' He straightened, holding rein on his patience. 'Soon's you boys get Red to the doc, let Prentice know what went on here. And be damn sure you tell what Red said about who done the shooting.'

The wagon was out of sight, and Tavener had the cigarette down to his fingers when Royal Janner came to join him on the veranda.

'Everyone gone?'

Tavener flicked the butt out into the yard. 'Uh-huh. Only a matter of time before the bastard's brought back, strung over a saddle.'

More by instinct than anything else, O'Grady found himself pointed back the way he'd come, headed for higher ground and the long-abandoned mining site where he'd been camped. Still way ahead of the search party spreading out behind him, he brought the sorrel to a halt, allowing it an opportunity to blow. Twisting around, he listened to the muted noises from below, gauging the distance still standing between himself and the riders coming up in the rear.

It sounded as if every Slash hand was out there, none bothering to conceal the fact. Getting dressed, saddling horses, determining the direction he'd taken had delayed them, and for now that put time on his side. But, if somehow they were able to create a wide enough circle, the chances of meeting up with some of them would quickly shift in their favour.

As if waiting until he was again moving, a question McQuade had asked pushed itself to the top of every-thing else on his mind. But he'd given McQuade an answer, and so he let it go, reflecting instead on his motives for the visit itself. In retrospect, it made no sense. What had he expected? A confession to an elaborate frame-up?

Or – and this made less sense – had he simply been trying to convince McQuade that he was innocent of the murders of Allenby, Lennon, and Vinter? If so, what purpose would that have served?

All he was really sure of was that he'd given in to a nagging demand which promised something so vague it could probably be regarded as no more than a hunch. And a weak one at that. He'd learned little; achieved even less. If anything, with Red Scheil carrying his bullet, with a hunt party snapping at his tail, he'd worsened his position.

And still, though the reasons for it remained obscure, he could sense a purpose . . . as if fate had deemed such a confrontation necessary in order that truth might be finally exposed.

And then it was there – McQuade's question bouncing around inside his skull, this time turning his thinking in a new direction. Shaking his head, he hauled up sharply. In a bizarre sort of way it made good sense, and he wondered why such a thing had not occurred to him before now.

Deep down he knew the answer, just as he knew he could no longer continue along the trail he was following.

Once more his thoughts turned to Old Town.

Still in his nightshirt, Ham McQuade was seated on the edge of his bed, dried blood crusting the side of a face which, so drained of colour, was as pale as his moustache. A trembling hand lifted the glass of whiskey Janner had poured.

'How's the head feel?'

McQuade scowled darkly. 'A bullet damn near splatters my brains, and you ask a fool question like that? How the hell do you think it feels?'

Mel Tavener smiled. 'Yeah, must hurt some. You were out for more'n an hour. Matter of fact, everyone else figures you're dead.'

'That damn fool Scheil!' McQuade swore softly. 'He came close to making that a fact!' He took another pull at the whiskey. 'Where's he anyhow?'

Tavener told him.

'O'Grady?'

'Got away, but it won't be for long. Every man we've got's out after him, and they'll get him!'

'I wonder.'

Irked by the expressed doubt, Tavener asked, 'What'd he want with you?'

McQuade tried more of the whiskey, straightened up slightly. 'I think,' he lied, 'he was hoping to get you, Mel. Said he ran into Raiker, that Herb told him a few things concerning Tim Becker, about you and Janner killing him.' Eyes hardened upon the thick-waisted man. 'That true?'

'Well, now . . . how about you take a guess.'

McQuade's huge hand tightened around the glass. 'Damn you! I said I didn't want any killing!'

'Yeah, well Becker was a stubborn cuss. A bullet was the only thing he'd listen to.' The smile began to slide from his face. 'In any case, what you want and what you wanted's no longer important.'

'What's that supposed to mean?'

From Janner came a whispering laugh. 'Want me to tell him?' He came a little closer, forcing McQuade to bend his neck back a little so he could keep the man's face in sight. 'Notice how quiet it is? Nothing to hear but the wind. Also no one to hear what happens in here. And like Mel already told you . . . all the crew, they think you're dead.' He chuckled quietly, amused at his own thoughts. ' 'Course, Mel, he never bothered to set them straight. The way you looked, so still, head all bloody like that, they just knew O'Grady's sneaked in here and allowed you to die with your boots off.'

'Yeah,' added Tavener. 'Did us kind of a favour, you might say.' He resurrected the smile. 'I mean, everyone knows the way you two feel about each other, and already he's being hunted down for them other killings.'

'Leaving you with that partnership agreement,' McQuade growled. 'Ready to grab all of Slash.'

'First try and you got it, Ham.' Tavener gave his emaciated companion a nod, and Janner unlimbered his gun. 'Finish your drink,' he said. 'Doubt they serve that stuff where you're going.'

McQuade didn't move. 'Those other killings you just mentioned . . . Allenby and the other two. That also your work?'

'The hell with that,' Tavener grated. 'You don't want that drink, that's up to you.' He drew his own gun.

At the sound of the hammer thumbed back McQuade sighed heavily. 'Wondered how long it would take you to get around to it.' Setting the drink down on the table beside the bed he reached for matches and a half-smoked cigar. He looked up, his cold, derisive laugh rumbling through the room. 'You never were too bright, Mel. Go ahead. Kill me. Do that, and you trade everything for a hang-rope, you, Janner, and whoever else's been helping you.'

It was not the reaction Tavener expected, and he let it show. 'What the blue blazes you talking about?'

Taking longer than was needed to get the cigar lighted, McQuade aimed a slow stream of smoke at Tavener.

'Just this, Mel. Same time I had that agreement of ours drawn up I had another document prepared. Thing called an affidavit, a signed and legally witnessed statement which, should I expire from anything but old age, goes straight to Judge Sunderson, or whoever's in his chair at the time. It names the most likely one to've killed me, and the reason for his doing so. It's also backed with enough facts to prove my charges.' McQuade drew deeply on the cigar, exhaled, and took another leisurely draw. Smoothing down his moustache, he offered the pair standing over him a smile minus any semblance of warmth.

Tavener sneered broadly. 'Expect me to believe a story like that?'

Wincing as he did so, McQuade rose from the bed. If he cut a ridiculous figure, this giant of a man in flannel nightdress, Tavener and Janner seemed not to notice.

'Got the guts to find out?'

Tavener opened his mouth to speak, and got no farther than that. Slowly he eased down the hammer, dropped the angle of the pointing gun.

His laugh riding a ragged plume of smoke, McQuade said, 'Seems to me, Mel, we could be partners for a long time yet. Or,' he added, tightly, 'until you try something stupid.'

19

With forced patience O'Grady watched the sun's slow descent behind the jagged ridges of the Sentinels. Not since prison had he known a day so long.

There'd been little trouble getting away from Slash's riders, though it took much of what was left of the previous night to do so. It could have been their inability to pick up his tracks in the dark that had gradually increased the distance between them, or maybe it was just the need of sleep that eventually blunted their enthusiasm for the chase. Whichever, after a couple of hours he was again down in the basin. A while later he was entering the wide, weed infested street bisecting Old Town.

The dull throbbing in his injured arm hadn't helped speed up the hours either. Twice during the day he'd bathed the wound in cold water, not caring much for the look of it, using the last remnant of his spare shirt to fashion a fresh bandage.

The doorless entrance to what once had been a store provided protection from the wind which, instead of subsiding, had gathered intensity, forcing the temperature down. Huddled in his deerskin jacket, his back against the sun-bleached door frame, he sat on a crate, chewing a piece of jerky, the last of the meagre rations snatched up when leaving Shamrock.

He'd tried to get in some sleep, but the nagging ache, the wind's persistent wailing as it wrenched creaks from old timbers, angry flapping from a nearby tin roof, and the need to be alert for unexpected or unwelcome company, denied him much success.

Only when night's dark blanket was fully spread did he go to where the sorrel was sheltered and, hoping the one townsman he believed could be trusted would not let him down, made ready to ride. What he intended remained no more than a vague idea.

Probably, because of the buildings and the fact that the town was built at the base of low hills, the wind appeared to have died down. For mid-week an unusual number of horses were at the racks, the music and noise from the Ten Spot equal to that of any Saturday night. O'Grady kept to the shadows of the back streets, his plans still sketchy.

Leaving the horse in a narrow alley alongside the house in which Doctor Samuel Brophy lived and conducted his practice, he made his way to the back, grateful to find the dim glow of light behind closed curtains. He stopped at the side of the building when he heard what sounded like Doc's voice. Then another, belonging to someone to whom he'd been devoting considerable thought.

He continued on toward the street.

'No,' he heard Susan Blayne say. 'You're tired and it's only a short walk home. I'll be fine.'

Brophy's renewed protest ended with a sideways

jerk of his grey head and a quiet gasp. 'Saints alive,'
he whispered hoarsely. 'Are you insane?'

Susan heeled about sharply, in time to see a shad-
owy figure emerge from around the corner of the
house. Greeting her with a quick nod, O'Grady
turned back to Brophy. 'Need to see you, Doc.'

'Are you crazy?' Brophy hissed. 'Everybody and his
third cousin's in town, still talking about getting you
fitted with a California collar!'

'Doc's right,' Susan said, glancing quickly over her
shoulder, and in just those two words could be
detected the quick rise of fear.

'I didn't kill Allenby, Susan. Nor the others.'

'We know that. But coming here—'

'Let's save the talk,' Doc cut in brusquely, 'and get
back inside. Too easy to see us out here.'

There was an uncomfortable warmth in O'Grady's
face, a slight burning sensation around his eyes and
a dryness in his mouth. He glanced at the freshly
bandaged arm and, with slightly more interest, at the
two pills placed in his hand.

'Just swallow them,' Brophy grunted.

Susan Blayne came forward, offering the water
she'd been asked to fetch. She'd been next to
Brophy when he'd cleaned and treated the wound,
recognized that which the medico discovered.

O'Grady returned the glass. 'Thanks.' His gaze
lingered, heightening the colour in her cheeks. She
was there, at that late hour, he'd learned, because
she'd gone with Brophy on one of his calls.
Returning to the surgery they'd found another
minor emergency awaiting them. 'You, too, Doc.' He
started to button what was left of his shirt. 'Got some
writing paper and a couple of envelopes to spare?'

Brophy eased him back onto the wooden chair when he tried to rise. 'In case you're too dumb to realize it, you've started a fever.' He nodded gravely. 'Uh-huh, there's some infection, and while I don't think there's any rush to buy a fancy pine box, along with those pills, you're going to take it easy until I tell you different. Got it?'

Susan watched the expression on the younger man's gaunt, unshaven face remain unchanged. 'And where do I get that?'

'Right here if necessary,' Brophy snorted, bulbous nose almost aglow. 'Or,' he added, struck by a fresh thought, 'I could get Josh to take you out to his place.'

'Of course!' Susan supplied eagerly. 'Mr Allenby was around earlier this evening, anxious to know if anything had been heard from you.'

'Trouble is,' Brophy went on, running fingers through his grey mop, 'the boy's still having a rough time over Arnie's death. My guess is he's probably back in the Ten Spot, and if that's so . . . .'

'Yeah,' O'Grady agreed, not letting him finish, knowing what he meant. 'Let's not intrude upon his grief.' He tried again, this time making it all the way up. 'About that paper . . .?'

Brophy's jaw tightened. 'Nothing I've told you has penetrated, has it?'

They stood aside, Susan and Brophy, giving him privacy while carefully he printed a message on a sheet of lined paper, sealing it in an envelope on which he applied a name. That done, he folded it in two, dug in his jeans for a coin, and put both items in the second envelope. On this was printed curt instructions.

Brophy watched him tap the rather bulky envelope thoughtfully against his thigh. 'Problem?'

Listening to the wind sighing mournfully under the eaves, O'Grady held his reply until finally pushing up from the cluttered roll-top desk. 'Sorry. Was trying to figure how to get this delivered . . . .'

Doc came and took the envelope, glanced at the message. 'Going to tell me what it's about?'

O'Grady hesitated. 'Sooner not, Doc. Don't want to drag you any deeper into—'

'Dammit,' the medico broke in loudly, 'you're trying to set something up! That's what this is all about, isn't it?' He drew back his arm when O'Grady tried to retrieve the envelope. 'Which means you know something.'

'No. It's just an idea that needs trying out.'

Brophy re-read the message. 'Who's this for?'

'You'll think I'm crazy,' O'Grady sighed wearily, 'but it's the best I could come up with. Figured on leaving it on the desk at the hotel.'

'That accounts for the money you put inside. Only what makes you think it won't simply be pocketed, everything else just ignored?'

'Not if it's Ozzie Framley.'

'Yeah . . . not knowing who left it, the squirt will be too scared of repercussions.' Brophy gave the envelope another brief inspection before turning to Susan. 'This,' he told her, 'is probably his only reason for coming here. Not for my professional services – not to have that arm fixed – oh no!' His tone gathered feigned disgust. 'All he really wanted was my help getting this thing delivered!' He swung back to O'Grady. 'Right?'

'Forget it,' O'Grady said. 'Guess I was being stupid.' He put out his hand for the letter, but

Brophy stepped back, thoughtfully massaging his chin.

'So happens you picked an opportune time. Got a patient at the hotel, someone you might even know. Big, red-headed feller, suffering some with a busted hip. Mighty be a kindly gesture were I to take over a little something extra to relieve his discomfort.'

Susan pushed quickly forward. 'Let me. I have to pass the hotel on my way home.'

'No,' O'Grady told her. 'I won't have you involved. Besides, it's late.'

'It's not that late. And – and nobody'd be suspicious. Everyone knows I'm assisting Doc.' Anticipating another objection, she took the envelope from Brophy. 'Please, let me do this.'

The fact that Brophy hadn't offered much resistance when relieved of the letter hadn't gone unnoticed. But before O'Grady could speak, Brophy had a hand flattened against his chest, blocking any move he might be considering.

'It's not a bad idea she's offering. Matter of fact, with her along, it could be even easier.'

'Then I'm ready whenever you are.' Susan smiled, quickly starting out of the room.

Sensing another protest, Brophy's hand pressed harder. 'Leave her,' he said, quietly, tightly. 'Can't you see? She wants to be part of whatever it is you're trying to do. And that, unless you're a whole lot dumber than I've ever suspected, ought to tell you something!'

20

'Carl Pickard must be a happy man,' Brophy grunted, tossing one of his disapproving frowns at the racket billowing out of the saloon across the street.

Head bent against the wind, eyes upon the horses lined up at the two tie rails, Susan offered agreement. 'He certainly appears to have no shortage of customers. Not if—' She broke off with a gasp, clutching at Brophy when a figure stepped from a dark doorway.

'Dammit, Dan!' Brophy snapped, himself startled. 'Lurking in the dark, pouncing on unsuspecting citizens! You got nothing better to do?'

'My apologies.' Dan Prentice lifted his hat, offering Susan an embarrassed smile. 'Town's busy tonight. Just keeping an eye on things, making sure nothing gets out of hand.'

'Which's why I'm escorting Miss Blayne home.' Annoyance remained thick in Sam Brophy's tone. 'It's been a long day for both of us.'

'I apologize again,' Prentice told the girl. 'But, contrary to what Methuselah's private quack might think, I wasn't lurking in the dark. Just doing my rounds, which includes making sure doors supposed

130

to be locked, have been and still are.'

'Sure, sure,' Brophy said with an abrupt change of attitude, anxious to be away and about their business. 'Kind of surprised us, that's all.' He took Susan's arm. 'G'night, Dan.'

Prentice watched their progress along the sidewalk, wind tugging at Susan Blayne's skirts. They had just about reached the hotel when someone crossing the street, heading in his direction, forced him to turn.

Coming to a stop, a grim-faced Ham McQuade plucked the cigar from his mouth. 'Want to talk with you, Dan.'

Prentice hitched an eyebrow. He'd known the rancher had ridden into town early that afternoon, but not that he was still there. Also, still fresh in his mind was the apparent, but inexplicable shoot-out between Alda and Drury, and their reason for killing Herb Raiker. *If* they had done it. He thought too of Red Scheil laid up at the hotel, of O'Grady's alleged responsibility for his condition, and he sighed deeply. 'Another shooting?'

'Concerns Allenby,' McQuade replied irritably. 'The dead one.'

The sheriff flung another glance toward the hotel, puzzled at seeing Susan Blayne standing alone near the entrance.

'Did you hear what I said?'

Prentice brought his eyes back to the man who towered over him. 'You were going to say something about Allenby.'

'And O'Grady.'

'All right: you've got my attention.'

'Wasn't him who shot Allenby, Dan,' McQuade announced slowly.

'I'm hearing this right? *You're* defending Conner O'Grady?'

Instead of answering, McQuade took a couple of puffs on the cigar, oblivious to the wind snatching a burst of sparks from its glowing tip. 'Night it happened,' he said, smoke slipping from broad nostrils, 'about the same time the paper says Allenby's crew heard the shot that killed him, I was there, at Shamrock.'

'You – *at O'Grady's?*'

'But he never knew it,' McQuade went on, remembering Mel Tavener wanting to know where he'd been the night he'd made the ride – the night Herb Raiker brought them news of the shooting. 'Had an idea about talking some kind of peace with him . . . getting a few things properly sorted out. But I got only as far as where I could look down on his buildings, and, well, I changed my mind.'

The lines ridging the sheriff's forehead deepened. 'What's that supposed to tell me?'

'That I was there; saw him twice come out of the house then go back inside again, at just about exactly when he was supposed to be settling scores with Allenby.'

Prentice released his breath. 'Realize what you're saying?'

'Only too damned well,' McQuade answered tautly. 'Spent a lot of time reaching a decision, which's why I stayed over in town.'

Unable to resist the urge, Prentice flashed another fast glance at the hotel . . . in time to see the girl emerging through the front door. Alone. His attention back on McQuade, he said quietly, 'You got something more to tell me, Ham? Like maybe the name of who it was really pulled the trigger?'

'That I don't know. But it wasn't O'Grady. You have my word on it.'

'Uh-huh,' Prentice nodded, gazing through narrowed eyes up at the bigger man's face. 'What I haven't got is your reason for at last coming to me with this.'

'Dammit,' McQuade snorted. 'I thought that would be obvious.'

'From someone else maybe. But from you . . . the way you been howling for that boy's blood.' Prentice shook his head, confused by McQuade's turnabout. 'What brought this on, Ham?'

McQuade sucked on the cigar, blew smoke into the night, and for a while Prentice thought he'd get no answer. Then McQuade said, 'Man sometimes gets carried away, I guess. Something happens and he sees nothing 'cept what he wants to see.'

Ozzie Framley was small and thin, with wispy blond hair and an Adam's apple the size of a baby's fist. Doc Brophy's arrival still had him quietly seething, unable to see or appreciate the reason for the medico insisting he be accompanied to Scheil's room. Especially when all he'd done was give that horse-faced brute a supply of pills. So why had it been necessary?

Framley adjusted his gold-framed glasses, lips pursing in a knowing smile. *Of course! The old fool had been afraid to go up alone! That was it! There could be no other reason.*

His eyes fell upon the envelope lying on the register. Before picking it up, he made one more adjustment to the spectacles. Odd . . . . It hadn't been there when he'd gone upstairs with Brophy . . . .

Which meant someone had come in and left it while he was away from the desk.

DELIVER CONTENTS — TONIGHT — AND THE MONEY IS YOURS

Ozzie read the message a second time, felt something solid under the paper, and reached for a letter-opener.

Inside was another envelope, this one folded. And a silver dollar. Framley flattened the second envelope between his fingers, cursing softly after squinting at the name it bore. If what he held had arrived just thirty minutes earlier, when he'd nipped out for a quick drink, delivery could have been so easily affected then. Why, he'd been within a few yards of the party concerned!

Wondering if the fellow might still be in the saloon, Ozzie Framley came out from behind the desk.

At the same time, Dan Prentice chose to come through the wide front door.

For no accountable reason the envelope suddenly felt like a tablet of stone in Framley's small hand.

21

Mel Tavener pulled his angry gaze back from where McQuade had joined Carl Pickard and two towns-men in a game of poker.

'Last one,' he growled, tipping the bottle, 'then we go see how Red's doing.'

From the other side of the round table, Royal Janner responded with a sneer. 'Don't see why in hell you want to bother with that stupid lummox. Far's I'm concerned, would've saved a lot of trouble had O'Grady's bullet finished him!'

It was the wrong thing to say.

'Watch your mouth, mister! Red's been riding with me since long before you showed up. As for O'Grady,' Tavener's pudgy hand tightened around the glass it held, a rush of blood bloating his face, 'that son of a bitch's already dead meat!'

'Hold it down,' Janner cautioned when a few heads turned their way.

'The hell with them!' Tavener retorted, but with reduced volume. 'Think I don't know the kind of stuff they've been saying behind my back? Joking about how that bastard got into Ham's room, right under our noses?' With effort, he let out his breath. 'OK! I've taken enough off of him. Next time we

135

meet, I put him under dirt!'

'More important right now is to calm down a little
and do some thinking. There's got to be a way of
getting around McQuade's set-up.'

'What the hell you think I've been doing?' Tavener
snarled, much of his foul mood still stemming from
the way McQuade had trimmed him back to size,
right when he'd been set to dispatch the old bugger
to hell. Or wherever else he was destined to go. He
hoisted the glass. 'Should've figured on him pulling
something tricky.'

At a table on the other side of the room, Josh
Allenby watched, wondering what they were talking
about, wondering especially about Tavener's obviously dark mood. Not that his own was presently the
best. Which was probably why he'd been left alone, a
situation that suited him just fine, for though he felt
need of the noise and activity of the saloon, he had
no desire for company.

Scenes of his stepbrother's burial continued to
pop up in his mind, intruding upon other thoughts.
He kept seeing Stacey, head bowed, shoulders heaving, sobbing behind a veil of black . . . and hovering
over all else, misty images of Arthur and May
Allenby . . .

He thought again of the reports he'd heard of
O'Grady's night visit to Slash and his wounding of
Red Scheil, trying to understand how Con had so far
managed to elude all those hunting him.

Unconsciously, he'd shifted his attention to the
poker game. Not a half hour ago, when McQuade
arrived, it had struck him as kind of odd the way he'd
pointedly ignored the man who, if recent rumours
were correct, he'd made a partner of sorts.

Josh swung his gaze back to the pair from Slash,

curious as to the way Royal Janner was leaning across the table. He wished he could hear what was being said.

Tavener, his own attention momentarily diverted, had himself not heard properly.

'That statement,' Janner repeated slowly, 'the one McQuade was talking about.'

'Yeah?'

'Said, in case of his untimely demise, it goes straight to Judge Sunderson, right?'

'Give me something that's new!' Tavener scowled, and downed the remains of his drink, automatically reaching for the near-dead bottle.

'So, in the meantime, who's holding the thing?'

Tavener's brows bunched together. 'Probably the damn lawyer that drew it up. Who else?'

'How about his pal the banker?'

A new glimmering appeared in Tavener's previously dulled eyes. If there was a document such as McQuade claimed, and it was in the safe-keeping of that milksop Terry Washburn ... well, then, maybe the problem wasn't nearly as serious as they'd been thinking.

Which was when the weedy figure of Ozzie Framley pushed timidly through the batwings.

Tavener's mind was racing in several different directions at the same time when, not long later, he and Janner came out of the saloon and unhitched their horses.

'Thought you were going to take over a bottle,' Janner shouted, pulling his thin frame into leather.

'Changed my mind,' Tavener flung back, pulling his hat down tighter on his head while backing the mare away from the rack. A sound almost lost in the wind had him turning. In the next instant he was board-stiff and choking. '*Sonofabitch!*'

Janner started a question that got nowhere.

'Look, dammit! Look!' Tavener spluttered.

Following the direction of the pointing finger, Janner was barely in time to glimpse a rider fast disappearing into the dark at the end of the street.

'I'll go to hell! Who—?'

Again he was given no chance to finish. 'It's him all right!' The words choked from Tavener's throat. 'Ain't never seen nobody else with a jacket like that! It's him! No mistaking it!'

Janner got his horse fully turned. 'Mel, leave it!'

'The hell I will!' Tavener flared. 'I been waiting too long for this!'

'Forget it,' Janner urged. 'It might not be O'Grady.'

'It was him, I said! Think I'd make a mistake like that?'

'He's probably long gone by now. In the dark, with the wind blowing the way it is, we'll never find him.'

'No?' Tavener sneered. 'You wouldn't want to bet on that?'

Janner stared at him, puzzled by the change of mood, the way the tension of seconds ago appeared to be draining away, leaving him nodding thoughtfully to himself.

'Yeah . . . yeah . . .' Tavener mumbled. 'It all makes sense now.' He smiled wolfishly. 'C'mon. I reckon I know exactly where we can find him.'

22

Once a hardware store, the second-to-last building at the end of the street was now but a wide, box-like structure, stripped of everything that could be used elsewhere. Inside, Conner O'Grady pulled his collar up higher, but it didn't help much. Battering the outer walls, howling through holes where once had been doors and windows, each blast of wind brought a fresh foretaste of a tough winter.

Minutes before, following a long, splintering groan, had come the racket of a wall or roof giving in under the onslaught. If, he mused sardonically, this was to be the night chosen for the flattening of Old Town, he'd picked one hell of a place to wait.

And for what?

Looking at it now, the plan he'd set in motion contained all the characteristics of something thrown together in haste and desperation, and which only a fool might buy. Or, he told himself, in an effort at reassurance, someone who'd schemed too long and too carefully to risk ignoring the note he'd sent.

His face was hot to the touch and in his mouth was the taste of gunmetal. One moment he was fighting the cold biting through his clothes, the next, resisting the urge to peel off his coat. He dug in his pocket, changing his mind when locating the pills. It could be that they were the cause of the drowsiness that kept sneaking up on him.

He shook his head, trying to lighten the sensation of cotton expanding inside his skull, to shut out the unholy symphony pounding his ears. Already he'd made mistakes and he could afford no more. When coming up with this crazy idea he'd overlooked something that now loomed as a major flaw.

Again he gazed searchingly along the length of the street, toward Tailgate. Scudding clouds put a heavy veil across the face of the moon, providing an opportunity for anyone exercising reasonable care to reach the abandoned town unobserved.

They drew rein near a scattering of spindly trees, branches waving like the arms of creatures enraged.

'Hell of a night,' Janner complained.

Tavener grunted agreement.

Tossing him a look that was wasted in the poor light, Janner said, 'Still like to know what makes you so sure he's there.'

'Because he is.'

'So what do we do? Ride straight in?'

Tavener grinned smugly. 'Sort of.'

'And get our fool heads shot off!'

'Nah,' Tavener said. 'Not his style.'

Shifting impatiently in his saddle, convinced now that Tavener wasn't quite sober. Janner frowned upwards. 'Then whatever you got in mind, let's do it.'

'No hurry,' Tavener told him, maintaining the grin. 'He's not going anyplace.'

'Maybe so. But take a look up there . . . give a listen.'

Tavener lifted his gaze, started a question,

exchanging it for a swift curse. Clouds still sailed across the sky, but with not nearly as much haste as previously.

O'Grady came awake with a violent jerk, his body bathed in perspiration. Clueless as to when the drowsiness had overtaken him, and with no idea of how long he'd been dozing, he sat very still, ears straining, trying to discover what it was that had whipped him back to consciousness. Then it hit him: the silence – or near silence.

The wind had dropped, become a rustling murmur!

He started to change position, to get the stiffness out of his back, and stopped, rigidly alert, listening again for something heard, a sound unrelated to the weather.

'O'Grady!' From further down the street of stirrup-high weeds, a bellow that reached his ears as no more than a thin cry. 'Show yourself!'

He shifted slightly, to see better through the hole that had once accommodated a window-frame. Midway along the other block he picked up vague movement, a brief, very faint glimmer of metal.

'It's me – Tavener! Come on out! I know you're here!'

Closer now, so close O'Grady could hear the muffled hoofsounds, the soft, occasional clink of a bit chain. He waited, and the rider, moving slowly, head turning cautiously from one side of the street to the other, continued his approach.

Unexpectedly, as if having caught the scent of another human, he stopped. 'O'Grady! You got any guts, show yourself, dammit!'

A coldness stirring in his belly, O'Grady rose,

seeing his plan already flying apart like a handful of sand tossed to the wind. He also knew Tavener too well to believe he'd ride into a situation like this alone. At least one more gun would be out there, covering his broad backside.

Mel Tavener nudged the bay onward, to the very end of the street.

Stepping over to what used to be the front door, O'Grady pressed against the wall at its left. Colt trained upon the blocky figure, he remained motionless, watching him bring the horse about.

Then Tavener was laughing, a peculiar taunting sound. 'Hey, McQuade says you been told something about what happened to Becker. That right?'

O'Grady answered him nothing.

'Answer me, dammit!' Tavener bellowed. 'You want to know what happened to the punk. I'll tell you!'

O'Grady's thumb curled and tightened around the hammerspur of the .44. He took a careful step, wary of what his boots might encounter upon the floor, knowing he could be inviting a bullet from a hidden gun just as soon as he showed himself.

Irritation and impatience and more than just a touch of nervousness lent a sharp edge to Tavener's tone. 'Dammit, you hear me?' He moved the horse forward a couple of paces.

'Far enough!'

Tavener reared back stiffly, hauling hard upon reins, not expecting any response to come from so close, yet still not sure of its source. 'Well, now . . .' he breathed.

'Stretch them!' O'Grady snapped.

'Hell, I thought you'd want to talk . . . .'

O'Grady's eyes were darting everywhere, trying to find proof of another presence, aware that the price of his next move might well be his life.

He watched Tavener's hands rise to ear level, was about to move again . . . and the earth performed a mighty lurch, almost sliding out from under him. A flood of heat rose up rapidly within his body, and reality slipped a gear.

It lasted only a moment but it left him wobbly, heart racing, not knowing what had happened, struggling to keep his legs firmly planted.

'Where the hell are you?' Tavener was yelling.

Using the inner wall for support, O'Grady swallowed. 'Right here.' His voice sounded so thin he doubted it had the strength to reach the street.

Tavener's head craned forward. 'Where? Come on out where I can see you!'

As if a hand at his back kept pushing, against his own protective instincts O'Grady took the step that would place him on the rotting plankwalk.

'I'm still listening.'

'Yeah, well . . .' Tavener shrugged, 'you want to talk. I'm not about to do it like this.'

'Mel,' O'Grady said, 'tonight, there's a few of God's creatures I like, and you're not one of them. Don't give me still another good reason for putting a bullet into that smirking face!'

'Problem is . . . you do that, you miss finding out something even more important.' Tavener spoke slowly, but his words had a hollow, breathless quality.

Now O'Grady knew he was right. There was at least one other out there, at this very moment probably positioning himself for an easy shot. There could be no other reason for Tavener's attempt to conceal the way he really felt under a façade of forced calm. Nor the admissions he'd made. He couldn't see the man's eyes, but when his head made a slight sideways twitch, there was no need to.

His own gaze swung yonder of the mounted man, at two buildings in a worse state than the one in which he'd taken shelter. An alley, faintly washed in silvery light separated them.

Hardly had he done so when, nerve ends pulling tight, Tavener let loose a yell, a frantic cry for action that had him turning on his heel, throwing himself into a crouch as he left the sidewalk. He saw Tavener's hands drop at the same time as a red eye winked from the shadows across the street.

23

Flame continued to spit out of the dark, sending lead zipping through space occupied only seconds before.

Three times O'Grady triggered the Colt, aiming at the powder flashes, each shot crowding the other. Above the racket he heard Tavener's wildly yelled orders switch sharply to violent cursing.

The thin, dark figure of Royal Janner stumbled out from the concealing shadows of a building on the other side of the street, narrow face turning to the heavens. He'd kept himself under cover while dogging Tavener, waiting for him to locate and lure their quarry into the open. Janner, the second gun, managed two more aimless shots before pitching to the sidewalk.

It was but a small beat in time during which it happened, but while it lasted reality seemed to slip into a haze where motion became sluggish. Vaguely he recalled harbouring the belief that Janner was both fast and deadly. He shook his head: maybe he was, and maybe Mel Tavener could be thanked for the outcome. Had his nerve held up, Royal Janner might be the one still standing.

A scream of unfettered frustration snapped everything back into focus. He swung towards Tavener who booted the bay into a forwards leap as he pawed at his holster.

O'Grady started to bring up his own gun, but already the horse was bearing down upon him. He lurched to the side, to get out of its path, and never quite made it. Flame belched down from above the saddle, but if lead found a place to roost, he never felt it. The shoulder of the horse struck hard, sending him sprawling further into the street.

Pain rocketed down the length of his injured arm when he used it to try and break the fall. He twisted, came down on his back, head bouncing against something narrow and hard. Half-stunned, he tried for a firmer grip on the Colt, discovered his hand empty, and saw a stocky silhouette lift up in the stirrups.

'Sonofabitch!' Tavener screamed, bringing the muzzle of his gun down for the shot that would end it. 'You killed Royal!'

The rest of his body held perfectly still, O'Grady's right hand groped feverishly among the weeds, but wherever his gun had fallen, it eluded the probing fingers. Wondering why it was taking so long for the shot to come, he threw a fast glance Tavener's way, and without understanding why he bothered when so little time was left, reached up to remove the object from under his head.

Instead of firing, Tavener remained motionless, throttling down a bubbling fury, the vision of Janner going down still vivid in his mind. It had shaken him because it shouldn't have happened. Royal was supposed to be good, which was why he'd been hired. But the fool had displayed only stupidity in failing to react fast enough when he'd yelled for him to shoot.

Tavener stared down at O'Grady, hating what he saw, anxious to be rid of him, yet freezing his finger around the trigger because there'd not be the desired satisfaction in killing him this way. Seconds dragged by. A moment before he thought he'd seen movement, but it must have been imagined, for there was none now. The bastard appeared to be out cold.

The wind, trying for a second breath, sent a withering sigh along a street growing slowly brighter as the moon poked its face through the clouds. Clearly now he could see the prone form flattened against the ground, hat pushed forward, the brim hiding eyes and the upper part of a face. A couple of feet away, the .44 that had brought down Janner.

Teeth showing behind stretched lips, Tavener allowed his arm to sag, took a grip on the saddle horn, and swung down.

'Can you hear me?'

O'Grady pretended not to. A boot dug at his ribs and the question was repeated.

'What are you waiting for?' he grunted, opening slitted eyes.

'Want you to see it coming, see who's giving it to you ... hear a thing or two before it happens.' Tavener's mouth twisted into an imitation smile. 'Reckon you heard half of Slash is mine now, huh? And that's just the start. Pretty soon the rest of the basin, everything McQuade's been too slow to take will also be part mine. Hell, maybe even *all* mine. Starting with Shamrock.'

'You the one killed Tim Becker?' The question rasped dryly out of O'Grady's throat.

'No, let Royal do the honours. Man was obstinate; needed some hard persuading. Nice clean job Royal

did, too – though Becker, he raised quite a fuss.'
Tavener chuckled softly, moved to the left and kicked
at an object that slid a short distance across the
ground. O'Grady guessed it to be his dropped gun.

Then Tavener was down on his haunches beside
him, forearm resting on a bent knee, weapon
pointed at O'Grady's skull. His free hand pushed
aside the hat so that he might enjoy seeing truth put
fear and angry hopelessness into those cold, glaring
eyes.

'This you're going to enjoy,' he grinned, and
waited for a response that never came. 'Always
figured it was McQuade's pup that shot your kid
brother, right?'

Watching O'Grady's jaw tighten, Tavener slowly
nodded. 'Thought so. Was all because of that
Brewster girl, but I guess you know that, too. He
couldn't take it, knowing Gil was beating his time
with her.'

Through tight-clenched teeth, O'Grady asked,
'McQuade know this?'

Tavener grinned again. 'Didn't when it happened.
Or any time during your trial. But he does now. That
is, part of it. Which's how come we're all of a sudden
partners. You see, Raiker and me, we were along
when it happened.'

O'Grady said nothing.

'Not that it makes any difference,' Tavener went
on, enjoying his own performance, 'but that night,
when we overtook Gil, on his way home, Lance was so
stinking drunk it was all he could do to stay in the
saddle.' Memory of the events seemed to amuse him.
'There he was, riding alongside the wagon, cussing
Gil, yelling for him to stop, and Gil not so much as
turning his head to let him know he'd heard. Then,

I guess, he must've had enough. He told young McQuade to go to hell, which really got the punk's cork popping. Suddenly he had that fancy piece of iron out of leather, and shooting.

'One of his bullets got Gil. Also got the hitch trying to break out of harness. He and Raiker had to dig spurs, ride like hell to—'

'You said one of his bullets . . . .'

'Uh-huh.' Tavener's grin widened. 'It's what I said. But here's the snapper, hot shot, and it's something only me and Raiker ever knew, and he's gone. It's the bit I forgot to tell ol' Ham. So listen, and listen good, because it'll be the last thing in this world you're going to hear.' To underscore the promise, he latched back the hammer of the gun. 'OK, after we get the wagon stopped, I check on Gil. He's bad wounded, but still a long way from dead.'

'So you rearranged matters.' The accusation was as cold and cutting as the blade of a peeling axe.

Tavener chuckled. 'Wasn't much else a smart man could do. To take him to a sawbones . . . risk having the boss's kid charged with . . . .' He shook his head. 'Uh-huh. That'd be real stupid. Next morning, though, Lance, he didn't remember a thing, didn't want to believe he'd killed anyone, let alone your brother. But he did, eventually. We came to an agreement, me and the kid – and it was just starting to shape into something when you had to come into the saloon, shopping for trouble!' Every vestige of humour had dwindled away while he'd been talking. Now, quite suddenly, the grin returned, full width. 'But then, things turned out even better for me, didn't they? Thanks to you.'

It was as far as he got.

Oblivious to the pain, taking the only chance he

had left, O'Grady flipped on to his shoulder, on to his wounded arm . . . and Tavener's trigger finger squeezed. Reverberating through his skull, the blast of the gunshot plugged out every other sound. Across his neck he felt the sear of exploding powder.

When reaching up to remove the thing his head had struck when falling, his hand had closed over what might have been a broken wheel spoke, or any of a hundred things involving a short length of hard, rounded wood. Clutched in his right hand now, he swung with every bit of strength he could muster.

The rounded timber connected with something solid, wrenching a dull cry from Tavener, driving him back on his heels. The gun tilted to the moon, reflexes tightened the finger wrapped around the trigger, and the shot shied off into space.

Amost blindly, O'Grady climbed to his feet, Tavener struggling to get up from the position in which he'd fallen. He made it as far as his knees, trying to point the gun when O'Grady let his club fall. He struck once more, and this time Tavener ploughed his face through the weeds.

Sucking air deep into his lungs, he stood, waiting for Tavener to make any move that would justify another blow. The ringing in his ear persisted, echoing like a muffled bell clanging from a canyon's depths.

It was the sense of movement, not anything heard, that brought him slowly around, grip tightening on the length of round wood.

24

'Well, now . . . seems like this time you needed no help from me.' He stood only a few yards away, smiling, gun held loosely, barrel slanted at the unmoving figure. 'He dead?'

Slowly, O'Grady let out his breath, relaxed his hold on the club. His head ached, his body felt as if it were on fire, and the sharp throbbing in his wounded arm was worse than ever. Carefully he bent to pick up his hat. Jamming it back on his head, he studied Tavener, sprawled belly-down, head twisted to the side. 'Reckon not. He's still breathing.'

'Lucky for him. Had you waited a second longer, it would've given me pleasure, blowing him away.' Demonstrating his contempt, Josh Allenby spat at the ground, then gave a nod meant to take in all of the old town. 'This where you been hidin' out?'

'For a while.' O'Grady saw where his Colt lay, and started for it.

'Leave it be, Con.'

He stopped. 'Got the note, huh?'

'And you're the one's supposed to've seen me kill Joe Lennon?' The laugh was cold and stabbing. 'What sort of price did you have in mind for your silence, Con?' He nodded slowly. 'Uh-huh, I got it.

151

Would probably've been here sooner were it not for
them two.' The gun barrel waggled at the uncon-
scious man. 'Weren't for his bellowin', might even
have rode in on them, got the same as whatever it was
they had in mind for you.' His sudden grin was mock-
ing. 'Man, that was really something, a note from an
unnamed jasper, claiming to have the deadwood on
me. Where'd you pick that one up? In a dime novel?
Or from one of your prison pals?'

'Does it matter? It worked.'

The response seemed not to be heard.

'Hell, nobody saw me smoke Lennon. Same with
Vinter. Nobody else around, just him and me. I made
sure of it.'

And there it was, the flaw in his plan: a confession
to the killings, but with no one else around to hear it.
Alone, O'Grady knew how much his word would
count for. Not that it mattered any more. The way the
chips were stacked, he wasn't going to be allowed to
talk to anyone. He said:

'No. In spite of everything you still couldn't be
sure. Which is why you're here.'

'Yeah, for a fact.' This time the laugh was brief, less
abrasive. 'Funny thing is, Con, soon's I read that
thing I had this idea it might be you behind it. And
the reason we're here, you and me, is 'cause somehow you worked things out. C'rect?'

'As will others, soon as the dust clears.'

'And how they going to do that?' The gun wagged
a silent threat. 'Before you answer . . . how's about
getting rid of what you're holding?'

Reluctantly, O'Grady let the piece of wood drop.
'Pretty soon you'll be inheriting everything Arnie
owned. The whole of the old Double A will be yours.'

'So?' The question dropped between them like a

fallen icicle. 'I'm the one who should've got what the old man gave Arnie! *Me!* I'm the one did all the damn work. Arnie that was mollycoddled. But I was just the throwed-away kid they took in, the one left to suck the hind tit!'

At no time could O'Grady recall ever seeing or hearing evidence to support that claim: it was something conjured up in Josh's mind, to justify his actions . . . to smother any sense of guilt. But there'd be no point in mentioning it. Not now. He said: 'There's more to it than that, isn't there?'

For a while it seemed as if there'd be no answer. Then Josh's face, growing slightly darker when the moon began replacing its veil, split into a humourless smile. 'Never figured you could read me that well.'

'Don't believe I ever did; not until now.' O'Grady held his gaze. Josh and Mel Tavener hated each other's guts, although they were alike in many ways.

'When,' he asked, 'was it you started getting ambition?'

'Not sure. Maybe when seeing McQuade move in and take what he wanted. Or maybe it was something I always had, like a thing I was born with. Only, with not a hell of a lot I could do about it, I never let it show.'

'When did things change? After you got a taste of what it felt like owning property?'

'The hell with that stuff! You were going to tell me how others would figure things out.'

O'Grady shrugged. 'Truth is, if it wasn't for McQuade, I might never have stopped to think about it that way.'

'McQuade? What's he got to do with it?'

'Nothing, and that's the point. He asked me what

he had to gain by Arnie's death?' Josh thought about it, slowly nodded.

'Uh-huh,' O'Grady said. 'You were the one who'd benefit most. But only if Arnie were to die unmarried . . . before he might make a will favouring a wife. Which is why you had to move fast.'

'Clever. But who'll believe it? Especially after I explain to Prentice how Tavener and Janner got you – themselves gettin' kinda shot up in the process.'

'The night I got back . . . .' O'Grady frowned. 'Was that for real, you following McQuade and his bunch up to the stage road?'

'Happened exactly like I said. Though, what I never told you is that, only when Janner dropped the rope around your neck did the idea come to me. Hit me like a falling rock, how easy your returning could be used to some profitable advantage.'

'And that, I guess,' O'Grady sighed, 'is the hardest pill to swallow. The way you set me up. The only death that counted was your stepbrother's. Lennon and Vinter – theirs were just part of your scheme to have the blame dumped on me, to make it look as if I'd gone revenge crazy.'

'Lennon and Vinter,' Josh shrugged, 'they were old, they didn't count for much. Their numbers were just about up anyway.'

'I was wrong,' O'Grady murmured. 'I thought I knew you, but I was wrong. You're the coldest bastard I've ever encountered.'

'Another thing nobody'd easily believe.'

'Won't they?' The question came from the thickening shadows at his rear.

25

The words were still hanging in the air when Josh whirled, veering sideways, firing twice at where he believed the voice to have come from, finding nothing except the dark, empty entrance of the building O'Grady had been using.

He choked loose a swift curse, but before another shot could be fired, O'Grady was crashing into him, driving him to the ground. Allenby let loose a wheezing grunt, managed to roll over on to his back as O'Grady reached for him. The gun to which he was still clinging swung viciously.

The barrel struck a painful blow, slid across O'Grady's shoulder and raked the side of his neck. Allenby pulled away, gathered his feet under him, and used the gun once more, this time glancing it off his attacker's head, sending him sprawling.

Allenby pushed upward, and the voice which moments ago had him throwing lead, shouted, 'Hold it! One more move and I'll drop you where you are!'

O'Grady, struggling to his knees, head in an aching spin, recognized the voice. Probably so did Allenby. But if he did, it meant something entirely different to him. He swivelled, fired, and this time the bullet found a target.

155

On the edge of the sidewalk, Dan Prentice was stopped in his tracks, slammed back against the building from which he'd been watching and listening. Allenby muttered something, turned back toward O'Grady, and wasted a moment firing a curse instead of the weapon. O'Grady, rising from the weeds, had found his dropped Colt and had it levelled.

Josh's next curse was drowned in the thunder of two guns firing almost simultaneously.

Not wanting to believe what was happening, he tried to check his backward stumble, but already his balance was going, legs unhinging.

Someone moved close by. He tried to lift himself from the ground, raise the gun around which his fingers remained fastened, but a hand reached down and plucked it out of his grasp.

'It's over,' O'Grady told him.

Dan Prentice said, 'Told you. I'm all right. Winded, is all. Patch-up I did ought to hold till we get back to town.'

O'Grady tossed a nod at the building. 'How long you been in there?'

'Long enough to hear Tavener shoot off his fat mouth, and all that followed. Came through the back way.' Then, seeing the next question shaping up on O'Grady's face, he said. 'That note. Saw Doc go into the hotel, the Blayne girl hanging around outside. Seemed strange, so after they left I moseyed on over. Caught Ozzie Framley about to make the delivery. Put two and two together, decided it was the girl who'd left it on his desk. Saw who it was addressed to . . . and just waited to see what Allenby'd do. When he left the Ten Spot, I followed, and found Tavener and Janner had got there first.' Prentice stirred irritably. 'Now go see if you can find where they stashed their horses. Time we got the hell out of here.'

It wasn't easy, but somehow they managed to get Janner and Allenby strung across saddles. Tavener, who came to while O'Grady was getting him roped, was able to board the bay with only minimum help.

They arrived late back in Tailgate, and for a while afterward there was a lot of activity, lots of questions. In the days following, even more.

Tavener, suffering only minor head injuries, and still protesting his innocence, was in jail, waiting to be tried for the murders of Tim Becker and Gil O'Grady.

Josh Allenby knew he was going to die, but it took him two days to do so. Towards the end, for reasons best known to himself, and in support of the sheriff's and O'Grady's testimony, he volunteered a sworn statement to the effect that he'd also been on hand to hear Tavener confess.

For a week the bank was opening late, closing early. Washburn, according to Doc Brophy, had been stricken with a severe attack of diarrhea. Why he kept smiling when disclosing this fact, few understood. And none ventured to ask.

Ham McQuade spent a long time in consultation with Judge Sunderson and the sheriff, then packed up and quietly departed Tailgate. But only after placing all his affairs in the hands of his lawyer, with instructions to sell off everything.

With one proviso.

In an effort to compensate Conner O'Grady for two years of wrongful imprisonment, and for the damage done to Shamrock, there was to be transferred to him certain land holdings, along with part of the Slash M herd.

Some said it was merely to salve his conscience to stay clean with the law, that he was only making an effort to square up for cattle stolen when trying to break O'Grady. Others maintained that, even if not directly involved, he had to bear some of the responsibility for the deaths charged to Mel Tavener.

O'Grady rejected the settlement, wanting nothing of McQuade's. Until Dan Prentice, Walt Denton, and the judge, sat him down and talked long and hard, until convincing him otherwise.

And that was it. The Allenby spreads would eventually be sold or auctioned ... new faces would be appearing in Tailgate, and soon recent events would fade into history, perhaps even from memory.

These were some of the things occupying Stacey Prentice's thoughts while she stood on the porch of the house, hands resting lightly on the rail. A lot of changes would be taking place in the basin, but of her own part in the future she could presently see little.

Down at the school she watched sunlight set Susan Blayne's head agleam when she came out of the building, Conner O'Grady climb down from the buckboard. She watched him go up to meet her, take her arm and lead her back to the wagon where they stood exchanging words none but they could hear.

Stacey Prentice drew back from the porch rail but continued to watch when Con O'Grady reached for the girl, drawing her into his embrace. When their lips met, Stacey went slowly back into the house, quietly closing the door behind her.